THE TEMPTATION

a kindred novel

THE TEMPTATION

a kindred novel

ALISA VALDES

An Imprint of HarperCollinsPublishers

HarperTeen is an imprint of HarperCollins Publishers.

The Temptation
Copyright © 2012 by Alisa Valdes
All rights reserved. Printed in the United States of America.
No part of this book may be used or reproduced in any manner whatsoever without written permission except in the case of brief quotations embodied in critical articles and reviews. For information address HarperCollins Children's Books, a division of HarperCollins Publishers, 10 East 53rd Street,
New York, NY 10022.
www.epicreads.com

Library of Congress Cataloging-in-Publication Data
Valdes-Rodriguez, Alisa.
The temptation : a Kindred novel / by Alisa Valdes. — 1st ed.
    p. cm.
Summary: Rescued from a car crash in New Mexico, sixteen-year-old Shane meets her soul mate, only to discover that he is dead.
ISBN 978-0-06-202420-6 (pbk. bdg.)
[1. Love—Fiction. 2. Ghosts—Fiction. 3. Soul—Fiction. 4. Dead—Fiction.
5. New Mexico—Fiction.] I. Title.
PZ7.V2158Te 2012   2011022939
[Fic]—dc23   CIP
                                                                    AC

Typography by Michelle Gengaro-Kokmen
12 13 14 15 16   CG/BV   10 9 8 7 6 5 4 3 2 1
❖
First Edition

This book is dedicated in loving memory to
Jesse Andrus and Mike Hillman.

THE
TEMPTATION

a kindred novel

one

The storm came out of nowhere. One minute I was driving along a desolate stretch of Highway 550 in the bright winter sunshine of New Mexico, listening to Vivaldi in preparation for my violin performance in Farmington that evening. The next minute I struggled to keep the car on the road, trapped in a sudden cold and windy blackness that had raced up behind me and rubbed out the sky.

Ice balls the size of frozen peas thundered against the metal roof. Violent gusts flicked the car like a toy along the empty road. There were no other vehicles on the highway. Not one. I was alone, miles from the nearest town. I'd had my driver's license for less than a year and felt panicked—I'd never driven in a storm like this. My heart hammered in a lopsided, urgent way as I tried to focus on what I was doing. I reminded myself to breathe.

I'd passed the tiny outpost of Lybrook ten minutes earlier, nothing but a couple of sagging houses and dirt roads. The nearest village was probably the puny town of Cuba, New Mexico, which must have been a good seventy miles behind me now. Farmington, a thriving metropolis by comparison but still pretty small as cities go, was more than an hour to the front of me in good weather. An hour felt like an eternity now. Nothing but gaping, vacant desert stood between me and Farmington, punctuated only by a couple of little settlements where you'd be more likely to find a rundown trailer with junk in the yard than, say, a hospital or gas station. I was in major trouble.

I vowed in that moment to always check the weather forecast before setting off on my own to performances with the Albuquerque Youth Symphony. I got into the orchestra two years before, when I was fourteen, and my mom had been ferrying me to my rehearsals and concerts across the Southwest. When I turned sixteen, my dad bought me a BMW and Mom started letting me drive myself to performances. I liked getting around on my own, but usually there wasn't an icy typhoon from hell bubbling up out of the yawning nothingness. In that moment, I wouldn't have minded having my mom there, or even my old, stained yellow blankie.

The noise of the hail scared my little dog, Buddy. He cowered on the passenger seat, his giant black bat-like ears flat against the small hard baseball of his skull, his enormous wet eyes bugging out. Then again, Buddy *was* a Chihuahua. The songs of birds on sunny days sent Buddy into the shakes. I teased him now, as I guided my car through the storm, trying to lighten my own mood with false bravado. "What are you anyway, a dog or a mouse?" I asked.

I should have pulled over to let the weather pass, the way they teach you to in driver's education classes, but I *had* to get to the concert. Tonight was my first public performance of the impossibly difficult and beautiful Vivaldi "Winter" solo as first chair of the orchestra. I had been working nearly twelve years for this day, and I wanted to show off.

So, I ignored the storm and kept driving, albeit cautiously, along that lonely, solitary stretch of the highway. The weather grew even fiercer, and began to crackle with electricity, tossing down blue and gold lightning bolts, thick and quick. The sky cracked open in a swirl of fast-moving thunderheads and unleashed an even heavier barrage of ice and blowing snow. I wondered if this was the stirrings of a tornado, the winds were so powerful. Fifteen minutes from Lybrook now, and the road was slicker, the sky was darker, the wind was angrier, and Buddy was a cowering, whimpering mess.

"It's okay, my little birdbrain," I cooed. "We'll be just fine. You'll see."

But I wasn't so sure. I kept feeling that there was something running alongside the car, but every time I looked over I saw nothing.

Buddy's eyebrows twitched back with anxiety. I called his name in a singsong voice, which usually drew from him at least a halfhearted tail wag. He remained worried, and looked at me with what seemed to be fear. I got the eerie sense that there was something other than the storm bothering him.

I felt the tires slide a bit, like the paws of a cat thrown onto an ice rink. That's when I saw an unusually large coyote in the middle of the road maybe twenty yards ahead. It was dark gray, soaked and sinewy. It limped pitifully in dazed circles in the center of the road, battling the wind and snow. I felt so terribly sorry for it my breath caught in my throat. I slammed on the brakes, which only made the car slide harder, sideways, toward the creature.

"No!" I cried out, in a panic.

The animal swiveled its head to look at me, as though it had heard my scream. In the split second before we were destined to collide, it . . . *smiled*. Yes, smiled—narrowing its glowing red eyes. Sinister, monstrous, and completely impossible. I yanked the steering wheel to the right, stomped again on the brake pedal. There was a horrible, deafening blur; a momentary sense of weightlessness followed by a terrible tumble and crash; a deafening crunch of metal and glass as the car flipped end over end, rolling off the right side of road, down the small rise of the shoulder. I didn't have time to scream, though I instinctively reached for Buddy to hold him in place in his seat. To my horror, I couldn't find him. Then the impact slammed me. The Vivaldi on the stereo stopped. Everything stopped. It was the worst sort of frozen stillness you can imagine, and there I was, wrapped up in it like a slab of meat in a freezer. I wondered if I was dead.

The car was on its side. The cold wind of the desolate northeastern New Mexico plains ripped through its hull with frenzied shrieking. I dangled like a puppet from my seat belt, disoriented, throbbing with pain everywhere. My shoulder burned, and something pierced my chest sharply with each inhale. My hands were cut and bleeding. My left foot felt unhinged at the ankle, as though something had twisted a large bite out of it. A cut somewhere on my head was gushing blood into my hair, into my eyes. I wiped what I could away, and squinted, but couldn't see or hear my little dog anywhere. I called his name. No response but the howling wind.

I suddenly remembered all those movies I'd seen where the crashed car bursts into flames moments after impact. I found the button to release the seat belt, and wriggled free. Be brave, I thought, or die. Gravity dumped me onto the passenger door, where my shoulder and back screamed with pain. After catching my breath, I managed to push myself out of the jagged hole where the windshield used to be, shaving off bits of clothing and skin as I went. I intended to run from the car once I was out of it, but the horrific pain—the worst I'd ever felt—limited me to a stiff, slow crawl. My legs simply would not support my weight. They were almost useless.

I blinked against the blowing snow and the oozing blood and inched away, breathing heavily. My hands and knees pressed through the snow on the ground, to the frozen sand and dead weeds beneath. A hot pain stung my back and shoulder with every motion. I was dizzy and afraid I'd pass out. But I couldn't let that happen. No one could see me down here, and if I passed out I'd freeze to death in minutes. I had to get moving, to keep my blood flowing and my body temperature up. With great effort I stood up, slowly and with a pounding, sloshing sensation in my head. Resting my hands on my thighs, I squinted hard, looking for my dog. "Buddy!" I called, my voice small and raspy.

I looked toward the road, but there was no sign of him, or of the smiling red-eyed coyote, or of any other car or living thing. I staggered away from the car like a horror movie zombie.

I scanned a nearby field and saw a small dark lump in the snow, maybe twenty feet from the car, on the other side of a barbed wire fence. I limped faster toward the fence, and squeezed my way through the wires, impervious now to the new cuts and pain.

Sure enough, it was Buddy.

I'd found my sweet little dog, the best friend I had in the world, covered in blood but still alive, on his side, licking his chops the way dogs do when they're hurt, his innocent black eyes searching my own for some sort of comfort.

"Oh, my poor baby!" I cried. "Good boy. What a good dog you are."

The effort of wagging his tiny tail to please me exhausted Buddy's reserves. His eyes rolled back into his head and his little body seized. In a complete panic now, I remembered my cell phone. I'd had it charging in the center console of the car, and now it could be anywhere.

"Someone please help me!" I cried, as loud as I could, my voice cracking and with the metallic taste of blood on my numb lips. "Hello! Help us!"

I stood helplessly at Buddy's side, my weight centered on the leg and foot that hurt the least, and I waited, but no sound came back. Not even an echo. My words were absorbed completely by the wind and snow.

I knelt down again, shivering from cold and pain but feeling it all less, now that I had someone else to worry about. The hail stung my numbing cheeks as I scooped Buddy's limp body into my arms. I worried I'd hurt him more by moving him, but I could not leave him to freeze to death here. I returned to the fence, ducked through it with my dog cradled in my arms. I tried to avoid nicking Buddy on the barbs.

I hauled Buddy to the road and wandered there, my pain numbing to a low, hollow throb, and I prayed for someone to come, some car or truck, anyone. I tasted more thick, metallic blood in my mouth.

The ankle gave way anytime I put weight on it. I suddenly felt thirsty, incredibly thirsty, dizzy, and faint. If only a car would come, just one car.

But no one came.

I realized that to survive I'd have to get myself back to Lybrook, and pray that someone was home in one of that town's isolated houses. Ten minutes by car would mean limping for hours. It was so cold. But there was no other choice. Better to die trying than to just give up.

I hobbled back to the car, which had not exploded after all, to see if I could find my coat and phone.

My parka, which I'd thrown onto the passenger seat when I started the journey, was tangled around the steering wheel. I tugged it loose with great effort and excruciating pain and draped it over my shoulders with Buddy in my arms beneath it. I tried to find my cell phone, but with a thud of dread I realized it was gone.

As I turned toward the road, a dark gray blur loped across the highway and disappeared on the other side with a soft rustling noise. Red eyes glowed out at me from the scrub brush and then disappeared in the darkness. A coyote howled, close . . . too close. It wasn't the sorrowful wail of an injured animal. It was something else, something terrifying, answered by something equally terrifying in the distance, as a pack heeded the call, and approached.

When you grow up in the high desert, on the outskirts of a big Southwestern city, as I had, you quickly come to know what various coyote calls mean—and why you should keep your cats and small dogs indoors no matter how loudly they might protest. I had lost exactly three cats to coyotes, and I knew precisely what these bloodcurdling yelps and howls meant. The pack was on the hunt and they had found food.

two

I hunched against the numbing wind. I heard the baying of coyotes getting closer, and I wanted to throw up.

Weakly, I scanned the ground for something—anything—that I might be able to use against them. But there was nothing—no stick, no branch, no rock visible above the thickening white blanket of snow. Nothing but three coyotes cresting a nearby hill, ragged and lean, their shiny eyes focused on me through the snow. They moved fast to hide themselves behind a bush across the road, next to a couple of wooden roadside crosses, the kind people made to mark spots where people had died, usually in car accidents—much, I thought hopelessly, like this one. Not comforting. Not comforting at all.

"This isn't happening," I moaned as I stumbled along

near the demolished corpse of my car. The heap of twisted black metal was the only shelter around, and I hoped that the clicking, gurgling sounds it still made, and the awful oily smell it gave off, might be enough to keep the animals away. It was far too twisted and crunched up for me to get back inside, so I could only use it for support.

The car didn't stop the coyotes, however. They inched closer, noses to the ground. Within a minute or two, I was being circled by a mangy pack of six or seven of them. They did hungry laps around me, coming closer and closer, communicating with one another in body language, with their eyes, and with those horrible, mournful yelps. Each of them, other than the red-eyed one, was smaller than a German shepherd, but they were strong and well-muscled, and in the winter, out here in the middle of nowhere, probably hungry. They would take what they could find, and right now the hot red scent of our blood must have been carried to them on the wind, delicious, seductive, irresistible as life itself.

Frantically, I tried to find something, anything, that had spilled from the wreckage of the car that I might use to scare them off. All I found were a couple of dirty paper coffee cups. I grabbed one of the cups, and wadded it up in my free hand, still holding Buddy with the other. The movement was excruciating, and I began to weep. The coyotes continued to circle me, growing ever closer, howling ever louder, their tongues wagging from their mouths in anticipation of fresh meat.

"Get away from me!" I screamed, hurling the cup at one of them as it slinked within a few feet. It scampered back, surprised for a second. Then it picked the cup up in its jaws, chewed it a couple of times, and dropped it in disgust.

Closer they came, all of them together, their hackles raised, and their lips pulled back to reveal sharp, serious fangs dripping with saliva. They snarled, and positioned themselves for attack.

"Go away!" I screamed again. I grabbed whatever I could, more of the cups, snowballs, and I hurled with what little strength I had left, first to the front of me, and then to the back. This wasn't how it was supposed to end.

Suddenly, two coyotes came at us with lightning speed, their jaws open and ready. I managed to feebly knee one of them in the head before it sank its teeth into me, causing a hollow pop, and the creature backed off, shaking its head. Unfortunately, the other coyote had already clamped its fangs down upon one of Buddy's back legs, and was attempting to drag him away from me. Buddy made an awful, desperate bleating sound I had never heard from him before. I was horrified and sickened, and shocked he was still alive.

"Get away!" I whimpered, hardly able anymore to hold

myself upright. The coyote would not let go of my dog. We were in a tug of war, and Buddy, poor Buddy, was the rope. I tried to hang on, but I was powerless and dizzy. I couldn't hold Buddy any longer. He began to slip away.

three

Just as the coyote was about to jerk Buddy from my grasp, I heard a loud boom. Gunshot! Instinctively, I cowered. The coyote released Buddy and scattered with its pack, but not too far. They still watched me hungrily from a distance, and began their circling anew. I tried to see where the noise had come from, but all I saw was snow and emptiness. I prayed the shot was intended for the animals, and not for me.

Quickly, the coyotes were closing in again, and the one with the red eyes came from behind me, charging with a terrible snarl. Again, the blast of a gunshot, and again the coyotes scattered, all except this one, who seemed utterly unmoved by the sound. I screamed, because the red-eyed beast was running toward me now, smiling as it had done in the middle of the road, leaping toward my throat. All I could do was stare, paralyzed by fear, as it sailed through the falling snow toward me.

Just then, I heard a different sound, a sort of fast *whoosh*, like a ball moving through the air. I saw a blur shoot past my head, and then the projectile, whatever it was, landed squarely between the red eyes with a loud crack. Stopped in its tracks, the coyote fell to the ground, a large dark rock in the snow by its head. Again came the whizzing sound, and a deep thunking noise as yet another rock found its mark. Again and again they came, in quick succession.

When the coyote had had enough, it retreated, loping unsteadily down the road with its tail between its legs. The other coyotes still circled, though at a greater distance than before. They would not give up easily. All around me I heard the whooshing noise, and watched as one by one the coyotes were struck and felled by stones. I spun around, searching for the source of the rocks.

At first I saw nothing, my vision blurred by blood and exhaustion, but then I saw the silhouette of a guy through the heavy snow. He was across the highway from me, on a small rise several yards down from where I was, atop a large, dark horse. His features were obscured by the snow, but I saw he wore a cowboy hat, and held a slingshot. He continued to pelt the coyotes with rocks, as the horse walked slowly closer. Finally, all of the coyotes ran from him in fear, back over the rise, and were gone. The horse clomped on, moving toward me, and stopped a short distance away. A powerful wave of pain doubled me over, and my vision tunneled. Dizzier than I'd ever been, I felt myself heave as though to vomit, but nothing came up. My chest felt broken, so terribly broken, and a loud ringing began in my ears. The world dimmed, and came back, then dimmed again, like intermission lights.

"You there, you all right?" called the young man's voice, tinged with a rural Western accent.

I tried to respond, but no sound came. I was weak. Breathing was incredibly difficult. The adrenaline had run out now, and I was overcome with a searing agony in nearly every part of my being. I leaned against the wreckage. My breath came fast and shallow as the world dimmed yet again.

"Hello?" he called.

"Here," I managed to choke out, my eyes blurred, the world spinning, the warm, horrible metallic taste thick and suffocating in my mouth. "I'm here."

The horse rounded the edge of the wreckage, and the young man brought it to a halt, swinging himself down off his saddle. He dropped the reins to the ground and said softly to the horse, "Stand."

It was an effort to keep my head lifted anymore, so

I stared at the ground, tired, so very tired. I watched as drops of my own bright-red blood fell from my head to the snow below. This is the end, I thought. This is it for me.

I heard footsteps crunching over the snow toward me, and saw his well-worn brown leather cowboy boots as he approached.

"It's gonna be okay now," he said gently, no trace of concern in his voice. "Help's on the way. Just try to calm down."

I tried to get a look at his face, but my vision blurred as I lifted my head. The ground lurched beneath me and I heaved again. "I'm dying," I moaned frantically between wretches.

"I won't let you die," he said, easing Buddy from my arms.

"Buddy," I whispered, groping in the air for my dog. I tried to see the young man, but my vision was still not right, and blood filled my eyes.

"Dog's all right. I got him. Try to stay calm. It's real important you do that."

The guy placed a hand on my shoulder and gently told me to relax and focus on his touch. I could feel the heat of his body through the frozen air. His touch gave me a strange and instant sense of peace in spite of all that had happened, and I felt my pulse slow down. For the first time since the crash, I was able to take a full, deep breath without immense pain.

He reached out to open my jacket, and I felt a literal electrical current course through me as he brushed against me, almost as though I'd been shocked, but without any pain. He reached around me, and placed his hands upon the bare skin of my back, along my spine, almost holding me in an embrace.

That's when I felt a buzzing inside my skull, a low humming sound as some sort of energy zipped out of his hands, through my skin, into my spine and on into the rest of my body. Suddenly worried as I realized this was not even remotely normal, I tried to push back from him. He held me in place, his grip nonnegotiable, and I felt his powerful heat and energy move through me, to my legs, directly into my broken foot, bringing relief with it. The pain began to simply drain away out of me, as quickly as it had come.

I was amazed and confused. "You're scaring me," I said.

"Listen," he said gently. I felt the electrical pulse again, mellower this time, and it filled me with the oddest sense of hope, and happiness, and calm. "There's no reason to be afraid of me. I won't hurt you. I'm here to help."

"But what are you *doing*?" I managed to ask.

I felt his mouth near my ear as he moved his hands to a different part of my spine. "Just shhh. Let it fix you."

"Okay," I whispered, feeling so strange and light-headed.

I wondered if I was imagining the whole thing. How much blood had I lost to be so delirious? And yet, the heat and his touch were so incredible, so welcome, so soothing, I couldn't help but feel a powerful happiness.

"That'll do for now," he said.

The guy released me and backed away a few feet. He squatted nearby and looked at me. I wiped my eyes, and it was now that I got a good look at him for the first time. He was tall, probably about my age or a little older, with an uncommonly—almost intimidatingly—handsome, kind face. He wore a heavy denim jacket, with a leather collar turned up against the snow. His head was capped with a cowboy hat the same pale brown as his boots. The handsome face was shaved clean, with a square jawline and a nicely formed mouth framed by dimples. He had a cute nose and large, intelligent brown eyes with incredibly long lashes. He carried himself with the rugged, countrified demeanor of kids from rural New Mexico, the type of kids I'd seen here and there all my life but, because I was from the city and came from money, never had any reason to talk to. I was startled by his unusually direct, almost grown-up way of looking at me. His cheeks were pink with the cold, and he looked straight into my eyes without a hint of self-consciousness, as though he could read my thoughts—or was at least trying to. He was unlike any teenage boy I'd ever known, and I can only describe him as seeming wise.

He spoke calmly. "Hey. I know you're scared. You're probably in shock, too. You got banged up real good. But it's all okay now."

Still unable to speak, I lifted a hand to my head and found the gashes there closed up. There was no new blood. I still had some pain here and there, but nothing like before.

He turned his attention to Buddy, on the ground at his side. He lifted him up. My sweet puppy was limp and unconscious, his breath coming in ragged gasps, his tongue lolling out of his mouth. The guy folded his strong legs beneath him, a calm yet serious expression on his face, and sat in the snow with Buddy in his lap. He ran his hands over my dog's legs and body, with his eyes closed and his forehead creased deeply. His lips moved silently as though chanting. He'd stop in a spot, hold his hands there for a moment, and then move to the next; wherever he'd been, it seemed the wounds just stopped bleeding and closed up. The coyote bite incredibly stitched itself together and was gone, just like that. Just like that, Buddy lifted his head and wagged his tail.

"But he was practically dead," I said, shaking my head as my body trembled with cold and nerves. "What you did, that's not *normal*."

"Oh, I don't know about all that. Depends where you're from." He grinned, and scooted toward me with a thoughtful expression on his face.

My head felt light with worry and confusion. I wanted him to touch me just once more, but I didn't understand how he did any of it, and this scared me. I began to cry again, a pathetic weeping that was involuntary and unflattering.

"Shh," he said. "I know it still hurts. I know. It's okay, I promise. All right? Everything's gonna be fine now."

His eyes were so bright, so soothing. He smelled dry and warm, like sunshine.

"What *are* you?" I asked. "Like one of those healer people they have in churches and stuff?"

He took a bottle of what appeared to be water from his jacket pocket, cracked the cap, and gave it to me.

"My name's Travis Hartwell. Here. Drink this," he said, and I did. The liquid—I do not believe it was water because it tasted like thin, carbonated honey—was warm and tingled all the way down my throat. Soon, my whole body vibrated with warmth.

He told me to concentrate, and next put his hands over the spot that still hurt on my shoulder, closing his eyes again with that intense look on his face. His lips moved once more, and I felt a soft, powerful heat radiating from his hands, deeper down into my muscle and bone. Thirty seconds or so later, the pain was half what it had been. A minute later, it was entirely gone. He repeated this everywhere I had pain, as though he knew where it hurt without me telling him.

I breathed out a sigh of relief.

He smiled kindly, and made long, direct eye contact with me. His gaze gave me shivers—the good kind. I didn't even feel the cold of the snow anymore, almost as though something shielded me from it.

"Glad you're feeling better, Shane."

"How did you know my name?" I asked, dumbfounded.

He ignored the question, and just used a white handkerchief dampened with a bit of water from his canteen to wipe the blood off my face. He smoothed the hair back from my eyes. He reached again into his jacket pocket, took out a bundle of small sticks tied together with string, and waved it slowly over the parts of my clothes that were soaked with blood. Most of the blood vanished, though not all of it. He moved the sticks over my head, presumably to take away the blood in my hair.

"This is impossible," I whispered, breathless.

He smiled a little. "I used to think like that, too. You'd be surprised."

I watched him wave the sticks over the bloody handkerchief, removing all stains from it before he stuffed it into his pocket again. I was overcome with awe, and a monumental hunger for him. Now that I felt better, his handsomeness was undeniable, and hypnotic. My racing heart felt an intense, inexplicable longing that frightened me. He peeked up at me, caught me staring, and blushed a little before looking away.

The hail and snow began to taper off, and Travis turned from me, moving with purpose around the crash site, digging through the snow for sticks and twigs. He dried these on the legs of his jeans, and set them in a pile near Buddy, whom he wrapped in his jacket. He scrounged for rocks next, and made a ring around the sticks. He held his hands over the twigs for a moment; incredibly, sparks rained down from his fingertips, and in this way he started a small fire.

"Come, sit," he told me once it was burning brightly. "Keep warm."

I did as he asked, and he pulled me in close. He did not touch me in a romantic way, exactly, but it was caring. My heart raced, and I wanted to burrow into him. I felt his hands, large and powerful, and I nestled under his strong arm. The strange sense of peace and calm, that same low thrum in the center of my chest, coursed up and down my spine. I felt that he recharged me, the way you might charge an MP3 player. He gave me strength. I wanted to stay in his arms forever.

I looked at him, and he looked back. I saw in his eyes that he found me attractive, too. He seemed confused about this, concerned. For a brief moment, he lost the look of mature confidence he'd had, and seemed like any other boy who might be nervous about a girl he liked. We shared an incredibly awkward moment where it felt like we both had things to say that we couldn't, or shouldn't—and didn't.

"You live around here or something?" I asked, trying to break the uncomfortable silence.

"Yeah, I guess you could say that." His eyes dodged mine now. He composed himself and became again the confident young man who'd saved me.

"What are you doing out on a horse in a storm like this?" I asked, hoping to draw him out, make him give me some hint about how he was able to heal me and Buddy with his hands.

He seemed slightly defensive, but still patient. "Came up real sudden. Just got stuck in it, I guess."

"And just happened to be armed?"

"That's how we do it out here in the country." He seemed politely annoyed that I was prying, and then, just as quickly as he'd grinned earlier, he frowned, seeming preoccupied with something he heard in the distance. I strained my own ears, but could hear nothing other than wind.

He seemed to shake himself. "Um, so. Where do you go to school, Shane?" It was like when grown-ups try to

24

distract children with questions they couldn't care less about.

"Coronado Prep, down in Albuquerque."

He lifted his eyebrows as though mockingly impressed. "Pretty fancy."

I shrugged, embarrassed and uncomfortable. Coronado Prep was a fancy school, but I wasn't particularly proud of that fact. It made me feel weird to talk about it outside of prep circles, because the school was obscenely expensive and elitist, and no matter how hard I tried I could never find a way to justify having been born so lucky.

"You rich or something?" he asked with a slightly teasing gleam in his eye. "Fancy car, fancy school. You even got you a fancy little dog there." Buddy growled at him, and Travis laughed, completely unthreatened.

I shook my head vigorously. "He's not actually fancy. He's from the shelter. We're not rich, really. I mean, I guess my dad is. But I live with my mom. She's just a doctor."

He laughed at this for some reason.

I felt on the defensive, and continued to dig myself into a hole. "I have a partial arts scholarship—music. I play classical violin."

"Classical violin." His voice was teasing. "Fancy music."

I snapped, "Not nearly as 'fancy' as making someone better by touching them. How'd you do it?"

"Even better. You're a fancy inquisitor. Who asks too many questions for her own fancy good." He smiled at me again, playfully evading the question.

"Tell me."

Travis pointed to the wreckage. "Shoot. Must be nice to have a Beemer and go to prep school, huh? Me, I'm homeschooled, and when I do drive, it's just an old pickup truck. I play an instrument, too, kind of like yours, but where I come from we call it a fiddle."

He looked back at me for a moment, with a gorgeous half grin on his face, and I got the feeling he was being sincere and mocking me at the same time. He seemed like the kind of guy who liked to tease girls—the kind of guy who'd be fun to spar with, verbally.

"You didn't answer my question," I griped, unable to stop myself from noticing his mouth, and how kissable it was when he pulled just a corner of it between his teeth to stifle a laugh.

"I bet you got you a boyfriend at that fancy school, too," he said, noticing me noticing his lips, and smiling shyly as a result. He lifted one eyebrow hopefully.

I felt my cheeks burn with embarrassment. I wanted to kiss him, and yet his question had forced me to remember that I did, in fact, have a boyfriend, and his name was Logan. I wasn't incredibly excited about Logan these days, and had actually been thinking it might be time to break up with him because we seemed to have so little in common, but he was still technically my boyfriend, and this technically made it inappropriate for me to sit here lusting after someone else. Instinctively, my hand went to my neck, where I usually wore the antique gold heart pendant Logan had given to me for Valentine's Day. It was gone. It must have come off during the crash.

"Yeah," I said halfheartedly. My eyes darted around the wreckage for a hint of the pendant. Nothing. "I have someone."

Travis's hopefully raised brow fell in disappointment. "Not surprised, pretty girl like you. Must be guys all over the place after you."

"Oh, please. I can't even imagine what I must look like right now."

"You're a mess, I'll be honest. But I can still tell how pretty you are." His eyes strayed from my hand upon my neck to the wreckage. "You lose something?"

I nodded sheepishly. "A necklace." *From my boyfriend, whom I guess I care for, but whom I've never wanted to kiss as badly as I want to kiss you,* I added silently.

"It'll turn up, I bet," he said. "Important things always do, if we wait long enough."

He shifted his eyes to the moody, darkening sky, and his expression changed to one of subtle anxiety. I got the feeling his last sentence meant more than I understood.

27

"Something wrong?" I asked.

He shook his head. "Nah. Not really. Just getting late, is all. I'm not supposed to be out after dark, but I can't just leave you here with Victor out there." He looked conflicted.

"Who's Victor?"

"My enemy," he said point-blank. It was a strange thing to say.

"You have an enemy?"

"Any man who stands for anything good has enemies," he said.

"Should I be worried?"

He shook his head after a moment of thought. "Nah. Don't think so. Last thing we want is you to worry after what you've been through. I'll handle Victor."

"Did you just say you can't be out after dark? What is that, some kind of curfew?"

"Scooter," he said, bucking his jaw toward the horse. "Some horses are good at night, but he isn't one of 'em. He's a good old boy, but he doesn't like the dark, and horses don't come with headlights."

I felt foolish for not having thought of that. In the distance, I heard the thwack of helicopter blades.

"You hear that?" I asked.

He nodded. "Your ride's here, I guess."

"Medics," I said. I looked at my leg, stretched it out

in front of me, and turned my foot this way and that. The ankle that had felt broken, ripped from my leg not long before, was absolutely fine now. Better than fine. It was great. No pain at all. "I don't really need them now. Miraculously. Mysteriously. *Explain.*"

He laughed at me again, teasing and confident. "Yeah, you do need that chopper. That car's not going to get you much of anywhere. Maybe a junkyard."

"Don't try to change the subject."

"Still, you better let them check you out," he said sweetly, standing up. Gently, he unwrapped Buddy and shrugged back into his coat, handing the growling dog to me. "I think I got it all, but you never know. I'll just leave you in their capable hands."

"How in the world did you 'get it all'? I *know* I was dying, Travis. And now I'm fine. How? You have to tell me! It's not fair."

He shrugged, and his expression grew pensive. "I just can't," he said. "I'd love to tell you, but I can't." He walked to the fire and stomped it out with his boots.

"Yes, you can. Come on."

"Do me a favor," he said, hoisting himself up into his saddle once more.

I waited to hear the rest.

"Anyone asks, you don't know who called nine-one-one, okay? Just say some dusty old cowboy with no teeth

29

or something. Don't use my name. Bad things could happen if you talk about me by name to the wrong people."

"What do you mean by *the wrong people*?"

"Don't matter. Just do me that favor. Can you do that?"

I nodded, intrigued and annoyed.

"Good, Shane. I gotta go now. Hope to see you again, though." He gave me a beautiful smile, and winked. "Never met a girl like you before."

The helicopter came into view now, just over the mesa on the other side of the highway, and Travis turned his face away from it anxiously, as though he did not want to be seen. He looked briefly at me with a confusing expression on his face—part longing, part anger, part sadness—then discreetly touched the brim of his hat toward me in a gentlemanly way before directing his horse to turn. Then they took off, fast.

"Travis!" I called out. "Wait!"

My voice cracked with emotion. All the love, peace, and energy he'd given to me seemed to swell up in the air around me and follow him. I felt cold, and alone, and terribly sad. It felt as though I'd just lost something very important, vitally important in fact. I wanted to see him again, and it was an almost overpowering urge, like extreme hunger or thirst. I needed him. I didn't want him to go.

"Come back, Travis!" I cried.

Travis didn't even look back, though; instead, he bent himself low over his horse, and together they galloped gracefully off into the growing gloom of evening, disappearing as mysteriously as they had come. He left nothing behind but newly fallen snow, and an ache in my soul as big and empty as the desert itself.

four

I knew one of the two paramedics who jumped out of the loudly roaring helicopter and rushed over to me and Buddy where we waited by the wrecked car. That sort of coincidence happens when your single mom is an ER doctor who doesn't believe in nannies, and you've spent most of your after-school hours for the past ten years doing homework at the nurses' station while your mother did things like remove bullets from drunk gang members. You know all the ambulance drivers, and the helicopter pilots.

This one's name was Jesse, a dead ringer for Ronald McDonald. He and the other paramedic—a tall, good-looking firefighter type I'd never seen before—were friendly, but all business. I faked a limp, probably because

I felt guilty they'd come out here for nothing now, and I didn't feel like telling them the unbelievable truth. They descended upon me, and strapped me to a stretcher and loaded me and Buddy into the helicopter with their heads ducked low. Before latching the door shut, Jesse jumped out of the chopper to pluck something out of the snow. He jumped back in a second later, holding my battered cell phone.

"Must be yours," he said.

I thanked him, and took it. Astoundingly, the phone still worked, and still held a nearly full battery charge. Predictably, there were calls from the director of the Youth Symphony, probably wondering what had happened to me. I texted to tell him I'd be missing the concert due to an emergency, but not to worry because I was fine. It felt creepy to tap "I am fine" into the keypad, because I shouldn't have been fine. I should have been dead. But here I was. Fine.

Jesse looked at me with puzzlement as the chopper lifted up.

"What happened out there, Shane?"

I shrugged. I had no idea how to talk about it, so I just looked outside instead.

"Seems to me you should be a lot more banged up than you are," he said.

"I guess." I couldn't look at him. I hate to lie.

33

"I mean, I'm glad you're not," he said. "Don't get me wrong. It just doesn't make a lot of sense, with the car like that."

I stared outside and hoped he'd drop it. A soft snow fell through the darkening sky, and I could have sworn I saw two red eyes watching me from a distance. I was hit with a sudden dread and fear, remembering what had happened and sensing from those eyes that it wasn't over, not by a long shot.

Shuddering, I pushed back the tears. As stupid as it sounds, I wanted to stay there in the middle of nowhere, because I wanted Travis with me. It was absurd, but I needed him, the way you need water after a long hike. Jesse busied himself checking my pulse, and with a shrug settled back for the very loud ride to the hospital. Buddy cuddled up against me, his eyes connecting with mine, and I had an eerie sense that he understood something I didn't, that he knew. He looked scared. Then again, Buddy almost always looked scared. I tried not to read too much into it.

Thirty minutes later, Jesse and the other guy wheeled me into my mom's emergency room at the university hospital. Buddy was hidden in a custodial closet by some nice nurses, because you can't bring a dog into the ER. It was probably for the best, because Buddy, even though he is small and cute, tends to attack people who aren't me. The only stranger I've ever seen him not attack, come to think of it, was Travis, at whom he only snapped.

Weird.

Getting wheeled around at high speed like some kind of invalid felt ridiculous and dramatic, needlessly showy considering that I wasn't actually sick or in any pain anymore. In fact, I felt healthier than I had felt earlier that day—and maybe even ever. I felt incredibly alive, energized, ready to take on challenges. Still, I was also heartsick. Who was that boy? What had he done? How, exactly, had he done it? How would I ever find him again to thank him? I realized I hadn't even said thank you. That was bad. Very. I am usually super polite. Hopefully he realized I was just distracted. I mean, I was sure he did. He seemed very understanding, anyway.

Jesse had radioed my mother ahead of time, to warn her that I was coming in, and sure enough, there she was, worried and angry in equal measure.

"Oh, Shaney," she sighed. "Thank God you're in one piece. We get more accidents on that stretch than we should. They're usually bad. They need to put signs up there, or flashing lights. Something."

"It's okay," I told her. "I'm fine."

"I don't know how she did it, Dr. Romero," Jesse told my mom. "That car was totaled. I've never seen anyone walk away from a crash like that alive, much less without a scrape. Guess it happens, though."

"I have scrapes," I insisted.

"I didn't see any," he said.

My mother paced alongside the stretcher as they wheeled me around a few corners, into a room with a pink-and-green-patterned curtain separating my bed from a bed on the other side. I couldn't see who was sharing my room, but I could hear the person coughing up their lungs, cursing, groaning, and begging God to help them—the usual miserable ER monologue.

"I don't need to be here," I told my mom in a whisper. I pointed toward the curtain. "That person? They need to be here. Not me. I'm okay. Really. I want to go home."

My mom smoothed the hair back off my forehead, and said, "We're just going to run a few tests to make sure you're okay. Sometimes, after an accident, you can feel okay but you're really not. It's the endorphins masking the pain."

Yeah, I thought. *I know all about that now.*

Jesse patted me on the shoulder, the shoulder that, an hour ago, had felt like it was torn from the socket and mashed through a meat grinder. He left with the other guy. My mom started to do all the things nurses do, brushing off the actual nurses by telling them I was her kid. She took my temperature by sticking an annoying thing in my ear, and got my blood pressure reading with the tight arm cuff. She listened to my lungs with a stethoscope. She checked my reflexes by whacking me on the knee with something that looked like a triangular rock on a metal stick. Everything was normal—except my mother, who was somber and not her usual wisecracking self.

"You seem fine," she said, hugging me.

"It wasn't that bad," I lied. I wanted to tell her the truth, but Travis had told me to tell no one. I was a little bit afraid of what might happen if I disobeyed an order from a guy who healed people with electricity from his bare hands.

"Did you tell Dad about the crash?" I asked her.

She nodded.

"Did he ask about the car first thing?"

Mom looked at me with the pained expression she got when she tried to protect me from ugly truths. "Of course he's worried about you. He's your dad."

"Whatever. He did, right? He asked about the car first."

Mom sighed wearily, her mouth a bitter white line. "Yeah, well. You know how he is." Mom and I shared a look of unspoken disgust for my father, who left us six years ago to marry a woman twenty years younger than my mom and start a whole new family with her in Santa Fe.

"I just want to go home," I said. "I really don't need to be here, and Buddy's in the janitor's closet. He might poop in there or something."

"What?" My mom perked up for the first time that evening. "Why is Buddy in the closet?"

"The nurses hid him there."

"You took Buddy to Farmington with you?" She was annoyed.

"I didn't make it that far, but yes, I took him."

"I told you not to." She scowled at me, and I felt grateful to be alive to experience this, even if it wasn't fun.

"He wanted to go," I said.

My mother rolled her eyes and, after a moment, sighed and patted me on the knee. "Well, kid, we should still run some X-rays and an MRI, just to make sure we didn't miss anything. You never know."

This was exactly what Travis had said, and so I agreed to the tests.

Two excruciatingly boring hours later, with Buddy now locked away in my mother's office, all the tests came back normal. I was starving, and trying to solve that particular problem with stale vending machine Doritos and a Sprite. I wondered just how long Doritos had to sit in a vending machine before getting stale. A century?

My mother hurried off to ask her supervisor if she could take the rest of the night off, to be with me after my accident. She said accidents can leave you shaken up and in need of rest, and all I could do was think to myself that she really had no idea just how right she was.

I lay there on the uncomfortable stretcher bed, waiting for my mom to come back and trying to ignore the violent coughing on the other side of the curtain. When the vile hacking and spitting finally stopped, I heard muttering, an old woman's voice. I was surprised by this, having imagined the disgusting, gruff cough belonged to a man. The lady was mumbling what sounded like biblical stuff, the usual crazy talk you hear in the ER. My mom liked to say that there were no atheists in the emergency room, meaning that in times of physical distress, everyone turns to God for help. There was no more religious place on earth than the ER. I tried to ignore the babbling, but one of the lines came through loud and clear, and spooked me to the bone.

"'Jesus went throughout Galilee, teaching in their synagogues, preaching the good news of the kingdom, and healing every disease and sickness among the people,'" said the mystery woman. "That's Matthew four, twenty-three. That's what the girl told me just now, the one with those horrible hands crawling around up there on the ceiling. She says someone here met one of them today and missed the crossing."

Gooseflesh dotted my arms. However crazy or drugged, she meant me! I knew she did.

She kept talking. "Then he called his twelve disciples

together and gave them power and authority over all demons, and to cure diseases. He sent them to preach the kingdom of God and to heal the sick."

My phone rang in my pocket just then, and I dug for it. I looked at the caller ID and saw nothing but a long line of zeros across the screen. This terrified me. I'd never seen anything like that on my phone before. Frightened by the old lady and everything else that had happened, I considered not answering it, but curiosity got the better of me.

"Hello?" I said, tentatively.

"Hi, Shane. It's me, Travis." He spoke as though it was the most normal thing in the world for him to be calling me, even though there was no way he could have had my phone number.

My blood ran icy cold for a moment at the unexpected sound of his voice. Then my heart began to race with excitement and fear. I felt a little dizzy.

"How did you get this number?" I whispered.

"I'm sorry," he said, able to project that sense of calm and peace to me now just through the phone. "I hope it's okay that I called you. Sometimes I forget how things work out there."

"Out where?" Goose bumps.

"In your world."

"What do you mean, *in my world*?" I whispered urgently, afraid of what he might say next. I freaked out now, as I tried not to imagine what his statement might have meant. What was he trying to say? I knew I had not given him my phone number. It was all very scary to me.

He said nothing, which was worse, in a way, than if he'd said something.

"How did you get my number?" I repeated.

"Same way I knew your name. It's all right. You don't have to be afraid. I just wanted to hear your voice again—make sure you were okay."

We sat there for a long moment, in silence. My heart pounded, and I was overcome with a fearful longing to see him again.

Thankfully, my mother returned at that moment, snapping me out of my trance, the keys to her Lexus SUV jangling with great practicality in her hand.

"You ready?" she asked. Noticing I was on the phone, she made a motion for me to hurry it up.

"So, yeah, you know, I'm fine," I told Travis, affecting a fake carefree tone. "Um, thanks for asking. My mom's right here, she's about to take me home."

"Okay, good," he said, and genuinely sounded relieved. "Get some rest."

"Okay."

Another awkward pause, this one shorter than the last, and then Travis said, urgently, "I have to see you again."

"Um, yeah, sure," I said nervously, scared and thrilled,

aware that I was limited by my mother's presence from saying too much to him. My heart pounded and my cheeks felt red. I knew I should have said no, because of Logan, but it felt right to agree to see Travis again—as right as breathing.

"I'll find you," he said.

"How?" I asked.

"Same way I got your phone number," he told me mysteriously, and I could almost see his teasing grin. "Bye, Shane."

"Bye."

I gulped, and ended the call. My mother, distracted by her own smartphone, asked me who I'd been talking to. I lied, and told her it was Logan, whose parents were friendly with her and socialized in the same symphony-and-gallery crowd. Saying Logan's name left a bad feeling in my chest; I recognized it as guilt.

"Oh," she said distractedly, texting someone. "He seems like a sweet boy."

"Yeah," I said unenthusiastically as I gathered my things to go. "He's great." But it was Travis's handsome face on my mind, not Logan's. "He's really sort of . . . magical."

"Praise and glory be," croaked the old lady. My mom stopped in the doorway, seeming not to have even heard the woman. Hang around enough deranged, injured people, you learn to tune them out. "'O my soul, and forget not all his benefits, who forgives all your sins and heals all your diseases, who redeems your life from the pit and crowns you with love and compassion.'"

I shuddered at the words. It was too creepy. It wasn't a coincidence, it couldn't be. My mom was still oblivious to the old lady. She ended her text, smiled as she waited for me to catch up, teasing, "Logan's *magical*, huh? Shane Clark, I have never heard you talk about a boy that way. You sure you didn't hit your head in that crash?"

"No," I answered truthfully, as she put her arm around me and we walked toward the exit. "I actually have no clue what happened out there."

five

It took the usual half hour for my mother to drive us from the university hospital where she worked to our four-bedroom adobe-style house set on its own acre of land in a gated part of the High Desert neighborhood. I was still processing the entire afternoon. It almost felt like I was watching my life unfold now from a great distance away, like things were in slow motion and I wasn't entirely inside my own body. It was all I could do to put one foot in front of the other and pretend to be normal because, let's face it, I wasn't normal anymore, and I probably never would be again.

My mother parked in the three-car garage, and in we went. After I'd showered—marveling all the while that there was not a single scratch on my whole, healthy

body—and changed into my coziest pink flannel pajamas, my mother settled me in on the sofa in the family
room, with a snack of cut veggies and ranch dip on a TV
tray, and more pillows and blankets stuffed around me
than I needed. I kept thinking I saw shadows moving in
the corners, the kind of silly imagined stuff that happens
after you listen to ghost stories at a slumber party or something. Every little thing made me jump.

Mom either did not notice my tense state, or she
pretended not to notice. She got into her own pajamas,
ordered my favorite comedy show on demand, and settled
in to watch it with me on the sofa. Mom's pager was blowing up, but she ignored it and finally just turned it off,
saying I was more important to her than anything else
right then. It was nice to hear that. Truth be told, it had
been a while since I felt like I came first before her job. I
was glad to have her home with me, but wished terribly
that I could tell her everything that had happened.

"If you want to talk about it," she said, staring at the
TV screen, meaning that she was there to listen and that
she had, in fact, noticed my uneasiness.

"I'm okay," I said, turning my attention from the TV
to Buddy, who was very much alive and well, and happily
lapping up the water in his bowl next to the refrigerator
with characteristic tiny-dog abandon. I smiled, but was
suddenly spooked by the sound of something bumping

45

around outside, near the trash cans.

"What was that?" I asked my mom, sitting up straighter.

"Probably just a raccoon," she said. "Barrels are pretty full—trash day tomorrow. Shane, you sure you're okay?"

I felt her eyes upon me now, and tried to compose myself. "Yeah. I'm fine."

"You know, it's normal to feel jumpy after an accident," she said. "It's okay, honey. Deep breaths."

I finally settled on the cartoon channel, something light and funny that my mom found gross, and I tried to distract myself from my fears with thoughts of how Travis had helped me after the accident. And the phone call. He'd said he'd find me. It was eerie but I felt, strangely, that the only way I could ever feel safe again would be if Travis were with me. It made no sense, and was all very exciting. I wanted to call my best friend, Kelsey, to tell her what had happened, but my mom was staying very close to me, hovering. Kelsey was the only person I could think of who might not think I was crazy. Then again, she might. I didn't know, but I did know I had to tell someone. Kelsey and I had been best friends since first grade, and no one had been through more with me than she had, from my parents' divorce to getting our first periods and training bras, to our first kisses from boys. We shared all our secrets, and had an understanding between us that we'd always be honest with each other, and never judge each other. I needed her now.

Suddenly, Buddy sprinted from the kitchen to the family room, hackles raised, and began to bark vehemently, spinning in ridiculous little circles as he often did when he grew overly excited about protecting us.

I froze on the sofa, goose bumps rising all over me, holding my glass of apple juice perfectly still and trying to hear what had upset the dog. I had a ridiculous thought, which was no less scary for being stupid: What if it was the coyote again? The one with the red eyes? What if it had come back to finish what it started?

"Buddy!" My mother admonished him in her usual way, clapping her hands together to get his attention. "No! Stop it."

Buddy ignored her and kept growling, furiously focused on something that seemed to be inside the house with us and not outside at all. He began to nip at the air, growling as though there were a man walking around in here. I'd never seen him do anything remotely like that before.

"No, Buddy!" my mother demanded. But Buddy didn't listen. He wasn't exactly obedient once he started whirling and barking.

"C'mere, little thing," I called him gently, fighting the panic rising in my chest, hoping that a little reverse psychology might work on my pooch. He gave me only a passing glance, his ears twitching madly, and went back to his frenzied attack upon the air.

"Probably just the neighbors coming home," my mom said with a roll of her eyes, rubbing her temples with her fingertips as though my dog gave her a headache.

I told her I agreed, but I didn't really. I had chills. I sensed it, too, whatever it was. Something bad was in the room with us. I knew it at a deep and visceral level, almost like instinct. I felt watched. But I also felt brave. Whatever was happening to me, I was not about to let it win. I was a girl who didn't back down from a fight when one found me, and I wasn't about to start now.

I set the juice glass down on the tray and unwrapped myself from the soft red chenille blanket. Whatever had been in the room receded with my getting up and mentally challenging it. I felt it go. It was so strange.

I padded over to where Buddy stood, and tried to listen to the outside. I heard nothing. I scooped him up into my arms, hoping to calm him down, but Buddy squirmed to be free. He wriggled out of my hold, jumping to the carpet, and rushed off down the hall, yapping all the way.

"Have I mentioned lately how much I regret getting that stupid dog?" my mother joked.

"I'll see what's bugging him," I said, my heart pounding with unspoken dread.

Mom said, "Let me go put some kibble in his bowl and

see if that gets his attention. I swear, he's going to get us a noise ordinance penalty."

I tiptoed down the hall to the darkened door of the guest room, where Buddy was going ballistic. I peeked inside, and felt the malevolent presence again. The curtains were still open from earlier in the day, and through the window I could see the blue-black sky, the charcoal outline of the mountains, and a few twinkling stars. I saw the juniper tree wave and bend in the wind. Nothing unusual. Buddy pawed at the carpet under the window, and growled.

"What is it, Buddy?" I whispered. "Who's here?"

To my horror, I was answered by a faint tapping sound upon the glass of the window. From the outside. Frozen with fear, but not about to be defeated by it, I strained my eyes against the darkness, and saw something moving out there, a dark shadow. It looked sort of like a man. I gasped, and ducked back into the hallway. I thought to call for my mother, but what if it was Travis out there? Hadn't he said he'd find me? Was he finding me already? Hadn't I told him I was going home? But why would he be here now?

A moment later, I sneaked another look, holding the smooth, plastered wall with my hands to steady myself. I saw nothing. For a second, I wondered if I'd maybe just seen a bear. Sometimes they came down to the foothills at night to root through garbage cans, especially on the night before trash day, when everyone's cans were stuffed with delectable refuse. I inhaled deeply to calm myself, and began to force myself to relax. But then something moved again, just outside the window, and I was pretty sure I saw two angry red eyes shining through the darkness.

I ducked out of sight again, my heart thundering madly.

"Mom!" I screamed. "Mom!"

I heard her stop pouring the kibble into Buddy's metal dish in the kitchen, and then I heard her come running down the hall. She was soon at my side.

"What's wrong?" she asked.

"I think I saw something out there," I told her, my voice quivering. "Outside the window. A, a . . . a man." But as I said the word *man*, my instinct corrected me. Demon, it said. I didn't know where that word came from, only that there it was, front and center in my mind. A demon was here.

Mom walked fearlessly into the guest room and looked around. I heard her close the curtains over the window, and she turned on the overhead light in the room. She returned to me, looking unconcerned about things that go bump in the night, but quite concerned about me. Buddy's barking had stopped, and he followed her, seeming perfectly relaxed and content.

"There's nothing there," Mom said.

"I swear, it was there. With red eyes."

My mother looked at me with pity, and rubbed my upper back. "I think you've had a really tough day, Shaney. You should try to rest if you can. Sleep is a great healer."

"A what?" I asked, the hair on the back of my neck rising. Was it another coincidence, my mom using the word *healer*, or was I so delusional that I was starting to see supernatural messages and meanings where there actually weren't any?

My mother stared at me like I was crazy. "Shane, why are you acting like this?"

"I don't know," I lied, not wanting to scare her, or to give her any reason to treat me like a lunatic. "I guess I'm just tired."

Mom put an arm around me, and steered me toward my bedroom. "You need sleep, pumpkin. That's all this is. You've had a heck of a day. Come on, sweetheart. Let's get you to bed."

I walked with her, and tried to still my mind, but the sense of dread only grew stronger with each step toward my room. This wasn't over, I realized.

Whatever it was, it had only just begun.

six

Sleep did not come easily for me that night. Outside was calm and quiet, but I had an uncanny sense that there was something out there watching the house, and me. My mom stood by the bedside, having just tucked me in like I was a little girl again. I pulled the down comforter in the pink striped duvet cover up over my ears, and asked her to leave my door open, with the hall light on, just as I used to many years before. She bit her lower lip, a concerned look on her face, and told me she loved me before she left the room. Buddy came prancing in with a tinkle of tags, and used the padded doggy stairs we'd provided for him to join me on the bed. Soon, he was snoring at my feet as though he had not a care in the world.

I was weary to my marrow, drained and physically

tired, but my mind raced a million miles an hour with thoughts of Travis. Silly as it sounded, I missed him. I needed to see him, urgently. It was impossible to explain why. I just did. I thought about his face, his hands, the sunshine smell of him, the masterful way he controlled his horse, his perfect aim with a slingshot. I wondered now why he hadn't just shot the coyotes with his gun. I wanted to ask him. There were so many questions. But even more than that, I just wanted to be held by him, to feel that incredible safety. I hoped he would find me, that I'd see him again. I thought of his beautiful lips, and imagined what it might be like to kiss them. If his touch was magical, what would his kiss be like?

I began to criticize myself for being foolish—was I just being a dumb, obsessive girl? There had to be a logical reason for everything that happened. Maybe I'd given him my name and phone number during my delirium. There was no such thing as magic, right? But then, as soon as I thought that, a newly awakened part of me protested. Don't doubt yourself, it said; what you experienced *was* magical.

After a time, to try to drown out my thoughts of Travis, I turned on the iPod stereo on the bedside table, and scrolled through to the *Holberg Suite* by composer Edvard Grieg, the Sarabande movement; it was a beautiful and soothing piece of music that I hoped would relax me, ground me, bring me back into balance with myself. I lay my head upon a pillow, closed my eyes, and controlled my breathing. I tried not to think of anything but the lush harmonies, the meandering melodies, the way the slow, smooth tones of the orchestra mixed together to create something emotional and sweet, gentle and warm. I was so, so tired. Very, very tired. And in love, most likely, with a complete stranger, who felt like someone I'd known forever. It was stupid! But it was true, too. I began to drift off, with Travis still on the edges of my consciousness, and I fell asleep.

The music continued to play, and I found myself inside of it, moving through beautiful, spiraling geometric patterns in bright colors, patterns that I intuitively knew and understood were actually three-dimensional visual representations of the music itself. I had never experienced music in this way, and was astonished by what I saw, and how it felt to soar, suspended by the vibrations of the notes, sliding down a bass tone here, rising through a violin passage there. I had a body, just like my regular body, and I was myself, and whole, yet weightless. I knew somehow that I was somewhere important, somewhere I had never been before.

The music changed now, to Tchaikovsky's *Sleeping Beauty*, a rich, thick piece full of harp strings gliding atop pleasant bass thrums, a waltz. New colors, new shapes appeared to reflect the light and happy notes.

Suddenly, I was pulled forward by the music into a shape like a honeycomb, and then was sucked into smaller honeycombs again and again, down smaller and smaller, yet each piece was exactly a copy of the whole. I moved with the sounds, pulled as though someone, or something, was guiding me. I felt the thrill of being on a roller coaster in my belly, and the joy of being without a care or worry. It felt, oddly, very similar to the way I'd felt earlier, when Travis had touched me, and I knew he was there.

The song changed again, to Debussy's *"Nuages"* from *Nocturnes*. It was a more haunting piece than the others, and the mood of the shapes and colors turned dark as well. I hung there, watching in amazement as the music literally built a world around me, enveloped me, moved me.

I have something to show you.

It was Travis's voice talking to me, with his rural twang. I looked everywhere for him, but could not see him.

"Where are you?" I asked, happy and surprised to find that I was able to speak.

Right here. Here with you.

"But I can't see you!"

That's okay. You feel me, right?

"Yes. But how?"

Because I want you to feel me. I want to be near you. I couldn't wait.

"Tell me where you are."

Far from here, and also here exactly. I can't stay away from you. I tried.

"Are you supposed to stay away from me?"

Probably.

"Why?"

Hard to explain. I feel something really powerful for you. I didn't show it earlier, but it's amazing, the way you feel to me. Like I've known you before. I didn't know how to handle it.

"I felt it, too."

I don't know how this is supposed to work, us being attracted to each other like this. I'm not sure it's allowed, Shane.

"Allowed? By who?"

I can show you. I don't know how to tell you, exactly. But I want you to understand. That's why I'm here. I want to take you somewhere.

"Okay."

I'll show you. Can I?

"Why am I afraid?"

Because this is strange. It's new. You have to trust me. Do you trust me?

"Yes, I think so."

Good. Then come with me.

I felt as though I were being lifted, as though he'd

swept me into his arms and held me the way you might carry a person. It was unreal, so strange. So good. It felt incredible just to be in his arms again. I never wanted to leave.

Just hold on.

I focused on the space where I felt him, and for a moment, I saw the air shimmer in his shape, as though he were made of lights. I saw that it was Travis. It was him, just made of light.

"I see you," I breathed.

He laughed, and his voice was sweet and kind. *Good. That's good. Let's go!*

We moved at an incredible speed then, me pulled along by him; we flew, dipped, glided, and stopped in what felt like the middle of a darkened sky, suspended like stars in outer space. We bobbed, weightless, and I felt intense, enormous peace.

Look. It's beautiful.

I turned back and gasped at the sea of blackness around me and the bright blue-and-white sphere floating below: Earth, illuminated like a jewel.

I looked at Travis inquisitively.

"Am I dreaming?"

No.

"Am I awake?"

I don't think so.

"I don't understand."

You don't have to.

Again we flew, this time around the great blue orb, at an electrifying speed, against the rotation. Finally, we slowed down.

Here. We're here.

The music faded out, and I felt myself pulled down toward the planet, and farther, through the atmosphere, down through the sky toward New Mexico and then closer in on the area near Albuquerque. We were still weightless, but I could smell the air, and feel the sun and the breeze. It was summertime here and beautiful.

Belen, he said. *My hometown.*

Down we went, through the bright sunshine of a typical summer day, toward the large parking lot of a grocery store. We slowed down now, and hovered twenty feet above the ground. All around us people parked their cars, pushed their shopping carts, talked with one another, but none of them seemed to see or notice us.

"What is this?" I whispered, worried that seeing us would scare these people.

They can't see or hear us, Shane. We can't affect anything here, either. It is the past. We can only watch.

"Like a movie?" I asked, noticing then how old the cars looked, and how dated the clothes everyone wore were.

Sort of.

I felt him direct my attention toward the front door of the store, where a handsome man who was maybe in his twenties, wearing cowboy boots and a white baseball cap, was walking out. He had a strong jaw, and he pushed a shopping cart filled with paper towels and diapers. A brown-haired baby sat in the cart's seat, babbling to himself. Next to the man walked another child, a boy of about six or seven, also with dark hair, dressed like a miniature version of the father. The older boy watched the man attentively, almost fearfully, and it was now that I noticed the man was angry, but making an effort not to show this to the children. Walking fast, he pushed the cart across the lot, toward a big gray pickup truck, and began to unload the goods into the bed.

My attention was directed now to a black, extended-cab Chevy pickup with six tires—four of them in the back, the kind that had the rear end jacked up like a stinkbug. Its engine roared as it sped across the lot toward the man and the children, kicking up dust and pebbles, and annoying everyone it passed. The Chevy screeched to a stop in front of them, and the driver revved the engine aggressively while loud, ugly music belched out of the windows. The man in the white baseball hat tried to ignore the ruckus and took the baby out of the cart. Then an arm poked out of the driver's side window of the Chevy, a shiny black gun in the hand.

The older boy screamed, "Duck, Daddy!" but it was

too late. Several bullets were quickly pumped into the man with the white hat. He looked surprised for a moment, and heartbreakingly used every ounce of strength he had to gently set the baby down on the ground before falling to his knees, clutching his chest, a bewildered look upon his face.

The Chevy sped off, and people continued on at first, unaware that a man had just been shot, because the ugly music had drowned out the gun noise. I felt sickened, and wanted to turn away.

"Why are you showing this to me?" I asked.

It's the first piece of the puzzle.

The older boy screamed out, "Daddy! My daddy's been hurt! My daddy got shot! Help! My daddy's hurt!"

The man in the white cap collapsed onto his side, and blood began leaking from his nose and mouth. His body convulsed. His eyes rolled back in his head. The baby stood watching in confusion, but the older boy understood, and tried to revive his father, kneeling next to the man and desperately crying for him not to die, his tiny hands and face covered in his father's blood.

A woman with three children of her own rushed to the boys, and picked them up in her arms. The older one protested, but she dragged him away, tears rolling down her own panic-stricken face.

"Someone call nine-one-one!" she screamed. "There's

a man hurt over here! Oh, these poor babies, these poor, poor babies!"

The woman ran with the children to her own lime-green minivan, and put them inside, while other people congregated around the man in alarm. Someone called for help on a pay phone, and a man tried to stop the bleeding. Another tried to revive the man with mouth-to-mouth. But the man was dead, limp as a rag doll.

"I can't watch this," I said. "Get me out of here."

You asked me how I did what I did. It's a long answer. This is where the answer begins.

"Please," I said. "This is too much."

Okay. I'm sorry. I thought you should know.

I awoke with a jolt then, in my own bed, drenched in sweat with my heart pounding as though I'd just run a mile. I heard the echo of my scream still hanging in the air. The iPod was off now, and my dark room was silent and still. The image of the dying man stayed with me, and every detail of the dream was clear in my memory. It was unlike any dream I'd ever had before. I was pretty sure it hadn't been a dream at all, but something else. A message.

Soon, I heard my mother's exhausted feet shuffling in their slippers down the hallway, and her sighing, and then there she was in my doorway.

"Everything okay?" she mumbled, rubbing her eyes. "I heard you scream."

"Yeah," I said, trying to hide from her the way I trembled with fright. "I just had a bad dream, I think. I'm okay."

"You sure?"

"It was awful, Mom. The worst dream ever."

She came over to give me a kiss, and noticed I was soaked with sweat.

"Sweetie," she said, "you don't look well."

I answered with tears flowing from my eyes, in a sniffling sort of voice, unable to shake the sense that it had not been a dream, that what I'd seen was real. "Can I sleep in your room tonight?"

My mom nodded, but her brow was creased with worry. It had been a good six years since I'd asked to sleep with my mother. Under any other circumstances, I might have been embarrassed about this; as it was, I felt nothing but anxiety, fear, and tremendous sadness for the man who had been violently murdered in front of his children, and for the children themselves.

As I followed my mom to her room, with Buddy at our heels, I was overwhelmed with a sudden, confusing awareness: ours was a dreadful world, with the constant potential for horrendous suffering and misery; yet ours was also an extraordinary world, filled with infinite music, kindness, love, and beauty. I'd always known bad things happened, but it had been something happening to other people, out there, away from me; in that moment, bad things happening felt intensely, terribly personal. I felt I knew that murdered man. I was more disheartened than I had ever been, but beneath that sorrow bubbled an insistent joy and hope that felt an awful lot like love.

Nothing made any sense.

I crawled up into my mother's high four-poster bed, and she got in and turned off the bedside lamp. We both lay awake, her listening to me, me listening to her.

"Mom?" I asked, finally.

"What is it, pumpkin?"

"Hold me like you used to when I was little?"

And, mothers making up a huge part of the side of the world that is good and right, she did as I asked, without questions.

seven

On Monday, after a weekend resting at home with my mother, it was back to school and back to life as I'd known it before the crash.

I drove from our house to the Einstein Bros. Bagels near my school, feeling very high up off the road in the Land Rover my dad gave me over the weekend to replace the BMW. My dad owned a luxury car dealership in Santa Fe, and had no shortage of showy cars to choose from. I was a little embarrassed about the enormity of the new SUV, which felt like a tank, but he had assured me it was the safest thing he had in stock.

I hadn't heard from Travis again all weekend, or dreamed about him, and I felt sad about that and not knowing how to find him.

Outside, it was snowing again. The Land Rover infiltrated the storm, churning solidly—almost calmly—over the road. Dad might have been a lazy parent in most other ways, but in the car department he excelled.

I parked, and dashed through the snow toward the bagel shop. My best friend, Kelsey, looked up as I entered the warm, balmy café. I'd texted and talked to her on the phone a few times over the weekend. When my mom had gone to the grocery store, I'd even been free to tell Kelsey all about what had happened at the accident, and she'd listened and asked questions. Like my mom, she'd wondered if maybe I had hit my head, but she was willing to give me the benefit of the doubt because when her grandma died, electric lights and appliances in her house had gone on and off on their own at random for about a week after. But, Kelsey had added, the imagination can also play tricks on a person when you are emotional enough; her parents were both psychotherapists, and this type of analysis was the norm for her. Still, it made me think. I had a very good imagination as it was. Maybe I'd imagined some of what I'd seen with Travis. Maybe the dream was just a dream.

She waved, smiling, from a back table, where she sat alone. She was effortlessly pretty, with wavy blond hair and sparkling blue eyes, wearing all black as she often did—training for when she finally moved to New York City to be a famous writer. I waved at her and smiled, then

65

made a quick beeline for the counter to order. I grabbed my bagel and joined Kelsey, draping my red peacoat over the back of the wooden chair. I hugged her, but shuddered in her arms.

"You okay?" Kelsey asked me, concern etched into her face.

"I feel like I'm going crazy," I told her honestly.

"Do you want to talk about it?" she asked.

I shook my head. "Just tell me something normal," I said. "Anything."

"Well," she said, still worried. "I was able to get that ska band we talked about to play for my Christmas party."

"That's great," I said absently.

"I still totally want you to play something on your violin, though."

"Cool."

"I'm sure you'll think of some obscure classical pagan holiday song."

I tried to crack a smile at the joke, but failed.

Kelsey continued, "Oh! And I still need your help figuring out how to decorate. I don't want to go too traditional and boring, but I don't want it to look stupid, either. My mom wants a dancing Santa and elves, but I was like, please, no. She still thinks I'm, like, six."

"Wow, lame," I said.

"No, what's lame is she's totally against having

mistletoe. What's the point of having a Christmas party and inviting Jackson Wyatt if I don't get to accost him under the mistletoe?"

"He probably wouldn't mind," I said of Jackson, Kelsey's latest crush.

"You'd think I asked Mom to make the guesthouse into a smoosh room or something."

"Ew?"

"It's freakin' mistletoe, not a box of condoms."

Normally, I would have laughed and come back with something equally inappropriate, but I felt distant, almost as though I were watching my own life from far away, and I squeaked out, "TMI."

"Hey," said Kelsey, her eyes concerned once more. "Seriously. You don't seem right, Shane. You can tell me, whatever it is. Might help to get it out in the open?"

I looked around to make sure no one was close enough to overhear us, and nodded.

"Okay. So, like, I had this dream Friday night," I told her softly, "and—"

That's when the door of the café jingled open, and my technical boyfriend Logan walked in. He'd been out of town all weekend, trying out for a junior national rifle skeet-shooting team. While this was surely admirable in some circles, his love of hunting was one of many reasons I had begun to grow uncomfortable with him. After dating him for a year, it seemed like his interest in blood sports had grown stronger and stranger over time. We hardly had anything to talk about anymore. I'd talked to Logan briefly on the phone yesterday, enough to tell him I'd had an accident but that I was fine. He hadn't asked too many questions about it before launching into a detailed account of how he made the team.

Kelsey looked up and saw Logan; knowing my mixed feelings for him and my strong feelings for the boy who'd rescued me Friday, she sang under her breath, "Awk-ward."

"Yeah," I sighed. "What am I going to do?"

"I don't know," she said sympathetically.

Seeing Logan now, I remembered again why I'd fallen for him. He was the hottest guy at our school. He was tall and broad-shouldered, with light brown hair, sparkling hazel eyes, and a smooth, intelligent face—phenomenally handsome in a well-heeled, Brooks Brothers kind of way. The first time I laid eyes on him, I was sure Logan belonged on a sailboat in a Ralph Lauren ad. Today was no different; he wore his yellow ski patrol parka, dark jeans, and shearling duck boots. He searched the room, and spotting me, his face lit up. It pained me to see him so happy to see me, knowing that I just wasn't that into him anymore.

I sat up straighter, and smiled at him, trying to seem normal. Logan was about to wave, but he was distracted by a person trotting through the snow behind him toward the door. Ever the calm, considerate gentleman, he stood back to pleasantly hold the door for the stranger. I swooned a little at his politeness, reminded once more that Logan was the sort of guy old ladies trusted to walk them across the street. He did have a certain charisma and charm, and probably had a great future in politics like his father, a state senator.

My jaw dropped when I realized that the stranger Logan held the door for was . . . Travis, dressed much as he had been the day he rescued me, and wholly out of place here. I gasped at the sight of him, and dropped my coffee cup on the table in shock.

"Shane?" asked Kelsey, setting my cup upright again before too much fluid slopped out of it, and mopping up the rest with her napkin. She put her hand on my arm in concern. "What's wrong?"

"It's *him*," I whispered to her as my heart raced with fear and excitement. "That's the guy who rescued me."

Kelsey's eyes lasered in on Travis, and widened in surprise. "Did you tell him to come here?"

"No! I swear. There's no way he could know I'm here."

"Are you serious?" she asked, trying to keep up appearances of normalcy for the sake of Logan, who was smiling at us as he walked to the line to place his order. Travis shook the snow off in the entry, his eyes scanning the

69

room. When he spotted me he grinned broadly, and his smile—white teeth and perfect lips framed by dimples—was absolutely stunning. I felt weak, and scared, and tried to understand. This was impossible, I told myself, and yet it was happening. It was happening. Again.

Travis walked directly toward us, removing his hat politely. I saw now that he had brown hair, cut in a stylish way. He looked good with the hat, but he looked completely amazing without it.

"Mornin', ladies," he said shyly when he got to our table, holding the hat over his chest. He smiled, in an embarrassed sort of way.

"Hi," I answered, all my panic suddenly gone. I felt the same warmth and sense of well-being that I'd felt the last time I'd seen him. I stared, mesmerized by the symmetrical, perfect beauty of his face. Again, I had an almost overpowering desire to touch him, kiss him.

"I'm Travis," he said to Kelsey, holding out his hand to shake hers, and I realized I should have introduced him.

"Hi," she said, shaking his hand and seeming every bit as much in awe of him as I was. "I'm Kelsey. Shane's best friend."

"He helped me when I crashed," I said nervously, my heart pounding. "He called nine-one-one. I'm very grateful."

"I don't mean to interrupt," he said, smiling at me,

taking something shiny out of his pocket. "I found this after they towed your car away. Thought you might want it back."

He let the gold necklace with the heart pendant unfurl from his fingers, and it seemed to glow for a brief moment in his hand. Kelsey didn't notice because she was too busy looking into his eyes as though she wished there were a giant mistletoe hanging over his head right now.

"Omigosh, how sweet," said Kelsey, sincerely. "You came all the way here to give her that?"

Logan came up now, holding his cup of coffee, and stood next to Travis. Seeing the necklace he'd given me for Valentine's Day, dangling in Travis's hand, he shot me a quizzical look.

Quickly and nervously I said, "Logan, this is Travis, he's the guy who called nine-one-one when I crashed Friday. Travis, this is my *boyfriend*, Logan."

I hadn't meant to emphasize the word *boyfriend* so much, but it just came out that way. I looked at Logan and said, "Travis brought my necklace back today. I lost it in the crash. Isn't that nice?" I was smiling way too hard to be convincing.

Logan still looked confused. Defensively, he moved to my side, and clamped his beefy arm around me. It felt wrong to be held by him in front of Travis, and I squirmed a little. Logan responded by gripping me more tightly.

71

"Where'd you find that?" Logan asked Travis.

"In the snow where she crashed. I went by there yesterday, and there it was, shining in the sun."

"I gave her that," said Logan. "It's an antique. Part of an estate sale from Valencia County. Worth a bundle."

Travis nodded. "I know you got it for her. She talked a lot about you after the crash." He smiled at me to let me know he was on my side, and didn't intend to make trouble for me. He handed the necklace to Logan and said, "It's real nice."

At the same time he gave Logan the locket with his right hand, Travis slipped a folded piece of paper to me with his left. Travis's touch, as before, sent a shockingly pleasant electrical current through my body, almost like a deep breath and a shiver combined. It felt so good. I closed my fist over the paper, not daring to open it now.

Logan didn't notice Travis's masterful sleight of hand, but Kelsey did and she looked at me in shock. My boyfriend just narrowed his eyes at Travis in a jealous, almost hateful way. Travis did not attempt to return the glare, or even acknowledge it. Rather, he gave me a look of understanding.

"I better go," he said. "Pleasure to meet you both." To Logan directly, he said, "Take good care of her."

He gave me a quick, secret smile. I smiled back, affection pouring from my eyes. I couldn't help it. I was smitten with this guy. It wasn't right, or logical, or anything other than what it was—the most powerful attraction I had ever felt for anyone or anything in my life.

Logan, seeing our exchange, let go of me and lunged after Travis, swiftly catching him by the arm.

"Yo, Stetson," Logan said, copping a tough-guy stance I'd never seen him use before. He puffed up his chest and stepped into Travis's personal space, too close. "I appreciate what you did here for my girl. And I'd like to give you a little something for your trouble."

Logan took his slick black leather wallet out of his back jeans pocket with great show and pomp, opened it, and flipped through the many crisp twenty-dollar bills he had there.

"Not necessary." Travis looked patient and unsurprised, his innate compassion evident and in stark relief against Logan's arrogance. He took a step back.

"Here," Logan said, trying to hand Travis a few bills. It wasn't nice, what Logan did; it was meant to put Travis in his place. I was sickened by the ugly gesture, and realized then I'd have to break up with Logan no matter what.

Travis shrugged gracefully out of Logan's grasp, ignored the money, and walked away. I wanted him to stay. I felt helpless and confused. My breath caught on the lump in my throat as he slipped out the door into the swirling snow. He shouldn't be going alone. I should be with him.

"You know," joked Logan, picking up the money from the floor, "you really ought to be more careful who you crash in front of next time. I think that hillbilly freak kind of likes you."

"Lucky Shane then," said Kelsey, her eyes narrowed in disgust at Logan. "He seems really nice, unlike some people."

Logan rolled his eyes. "Yeah, if you want to live in the sticks and your idea of fun is baling hay, he's perfect."

I hurried to change the subject. "How was the tryout?" I asked Logan. "Tell us about it."

"Oh, man," said Logan, quickly forgetting about Travis, his eyes lighting up. "It was awesome. I made the team, no sweat, but the coolest part was that at the end, I pegged a dove."

"Pegged a dove?" I asked.

Logan pantomimed shooting toward the ceiling. "Yeah, I was aiming for the clay pigeon, and then the dove just came out of nowhere and flew right in the line of fire, so I nailed it, and got the pigeon, too!"

Kelsey and I exchanged a look that was part worry and part disgust, masked by politeness. Logan kept talking.

"Just knowing I'd gotten it, seeing it fall out of the sky . . . ," he mused, with a strangely bloodthirsty look in his eyes. "It was awesome, that's all. It was like it was some kind of a sign. Oh, and look!"

Logan unzipped his backpack and took out a long rectangular wooden box. He opened it to reveal a huge, shiny silver knife, resting on blue velvet. It had notches in it, and was curved unlike any knife I'd ever seen, with what looked like an ivory handle.

"It's a bayonet military hunting knife," he said ecstatically, almost lustfully. "I've wanted one for a long time. Dad was so proud I made the team, he got it for me. The handle is awesome. It'll be awesome to use this someday."

"That's great," I said without any real enthusiasm. The knife scared me.

"Awesome," griped Kelsey, a vegetarian.

"Yeah, right?" said Logan, completely missing the sarcasm in her voice.

"Um, I'm sorry to interrupt, but I need to go to the bathroom," Kelsey announced, gripping my arm with her hand. "Shane? Do you need to go, too?" She gave me a look that meant she wanted me to come with her.

"Um, yeah," I said. "We'll be right back."

"Women," said Logan, again rolling his eyes as he shut the knife back into its case. "Never understood why you always go in pairs. Whatever."

He didn't seem to suspect anything. I was relieved, and got up to follow my friend.

In the privacy of the locked women's room, after Kelsey and I agreed that Logan was acting creepy, even

75

for Logan, we eagerly unfolded the note Travis had given me. It read:

> *Shane,*
> *I can't stop thinking about you. I hope you feel the same way. Meet me at the crash site Friday afternoon at three. Sorry about the dream. You weren't ready. Explain all later.*
>
> > *Travis*

I stood silently for a long moment, in shock. It had been real. The dream had been real? I'd known it was, but there'd been doubt, too—until then. He'd been there. It was right here in my hand, proof of it. My mouth went dry, and I felt weak in the knees.

"What is? What's wrong?" Kelsey asked.

I looked her hard in the eye, and squeezed her hand. "You have to promise you'll believe me, if I tell you something. Promise never to tell anyone else."

"I promise."

I told her about the terrifying dream, and how it wasn't a dream at all but something else, something I didn't understand, and she and I just stared at each other, unable to speak for a long moment.

"Do you think that was Travis who got shot in the dream, maybe?" she asked.

"No. It was a grown man, with kids."

Kelsey's brow furrowed, and she winced. "You know you can't go around telling this to anybody, right?"

"I know. But I swear it's true, you have to believe me!" I began to tremble, thinking she might not have believed what I told her. She squeezed my hand back to reassure me, but still looked very concerned.

She said, "I've known you ten years, and I know you're not crazy. But promise me you'll be super careful with this guy."

"Why?"

"Because, what if he's . . . bad? What if he's trying to lure you out there to hurt you?"

"Hello?" I cried. "If that was his goal, he could have just let me die last week!"

"It was really that bad?" I could tell from Kelsey's eyes that she doubted me, and my heart broke. There was no way to make her—or anyone who hadn't been there— understand. Tears formed in my eyes.

"I swear. I was almost dead. I was seconds from death when he—he healed me."

"Even if he did. Still. You don't know him." She was full of unspoken doubt, and worry.

"You saw him," I cried. "Does he seem bad to you?"

"No. He seems great, actually," she said thoughtfully. "Much better than Logan."

"I know," I said miserably. "It doesn't make any sense! I can't understand any of this, but I know that I'm falling in love with Travis, Kelsey!"

"I can understand that. He's hot."

"It's not just that. I feel something—this electric feeling. It's so peaceful, but so weird! I crave him now, all the time. I hate being away from him."

"So you're going back out there Friday?" she asked me.

"I think I kinda have to, don't you think?"

Kelsey nodded, the best friend you could ever have. I couldn't think of a single person other than Kelsey who would believe any of this, just because I'd said it. That's what best friends did: they believed you, against all odds.

"He's the most amazing person I've ever met," I said.

"*If* he's a person, you mean," she said, ominously.

"What do you mean, if he's a person?" I asked, overcome with a shiver. "What else could he possibly be? You saw him."

Kelsey answered by raising an eyebrow. It terrified me, because something in me knew she was right.

eight

My first class of the day was AP physics. Normally, I looked forward to it, for no other reason than that our teacher, Mr. Hedges, was so eccentric it was funny. But as I sat at my desk in the second row, between Logan and Kelsey, listening to Mr. Hedges review material for the upcoming final exam, my mind kept going back to the horrific dream about the murder. I shuddered, and stopped myself from crying. I tried to pay attention, but it was no use. I kept finding myself re-witnessing the shooting, trying to make sense of it.

The classroom was like most of the classrooms at Coronado Prep—tastefully decorated and high-tech, while still being comfortable. One side of the room was taken up with large windows, and my eyes kept wandering to the snowy scene on the quad outside.

"Shane!" I heard Kelsey whisper urgently. She poked me in the ribs. "That's you."

"Miss Clark? Earth to Miss Clark?" Mr. Hedges stared at me over the top of his smudgy black eyeglasses, his beefy arms crossed over his chest. His nappy graying hair jutted out in coils around his head. His dark eyes appeared tired. Altogether, he looked like a huge toddler who'd just been roused from slumber. I suddenly zoned back in.

"I'm sorry, Mr. Hedges," I said. "Can you repeat the question, please?"

"No problem," said Mr. Hedges sarcastically. "I'm of course *more* than happy to waste my day and the time of all your fellow students repeating questions that I quite properly phrased already, because *you* can't be bothered to pay attention to an education your parents are paying more for than most people make in a *year*."

"I apologize."

"Don't. Just listen carefully this time."

"I'm listening."

"Very well. Miss Clark, can you please name at least four natural structures whose growth pattern is dictated by the mathematical golden ratio?"

My heart rate raced in a panic. I used to know this. I hadn't thought about it in such a long time that I couldn't remember. I closed my eyes, took a deep breath, and tried to come up with the answer. I wondered if I actually did have a head injury. This wasn't a hard question! I could feel everyone in the room shifting uncomfortably as they waited for me to get it together. Then, I remembered.

"Um, a pinecone, a ram's horn, a fern fiddlehead, and . . ." I stopped. I couldn't remember a fourth thing.

"And?" said Mr. Hedges before blowing his nose into a well-used handkerchief.

"And I can't remember," I admitted miserably.

"And you can't remember," he repeated nastily. He looked around the room at the other students with his eyebrows raised in superiority. "Anyone?"

A girl I'd never liked much raised her hand in the front row, always eager to humiliate me.

"Reba?" said Mr. Hedges, nodding to her.

"A snail's shell, sir."

"Very good. A snail's shell. Yes. All of these structures grow in a spiral according to the golden ratio, which can be found using numbers in what is known as the Fibonacci series. We can see this relationship very clearly in the ram's horn, pinecone, snail's shell, and fern fiddlehead, but did you know that the same ratio exists in many other places as well?"

We all sat blinking at him.

"For instance," Mr. Hedges continued, "the ratio between the length of your hand to the length of your forearm is also governed by this same simple principle. So is the orbit of our planet. So are the relationships between intervals in music as it has evolved in various cultures all over the earth, with the pentatonic scale being always the first to spring up, because it is the scale you get when you divide a vibrating string exactly in half, and then again exactly in half, and so on. Nature is marvelously consistent, and it is these very same basic ideas that I am using now, in my work in quantum physics at the university."

Logan's arm shot up now, interrupting yet another of Mr. Hedges's monologues.

"Yes, Mr. Lucero?" said the teacher, annoyed.

"Yeah, um, you said you were, like, trying to find parallel universes, right?" asked my boyfriend, in a way that sounded clumsy to me.

"Not trying, Mr. Lucero. I have quite nearly succeeded. String theory is predicated upon the very real existence of parallel universes. It is no longer a question of if, but rather of where and how many."

"So, you're saying there are universes out there just like ours?" asked Logan doubtfully. He looked at me with an expression meant to convey his utter disdain for the teacher. I know Logan thought he was a crackpot.

"Yes. An infinite number of universes, exactly like our own, but also entirely unlike our own."

"That's cool," said Logan. "That's some total *Star*

Wars: The Clone Wars stuff, man."

I knew Logan was being sarcastic, and so did every other student in the room, but Mr. Hedges, the typical absentminded-professor type, so wrapped up in his own thoughts that he barely made it out of his head each morning, did not pick up on the mockery.

"I would have to agree," he said, rubbing his chin.

Though I normally found Mr. Hedges's rants incomprehensible, something about what he was saying made sense to me now, at a visceral level that I did not understand. My heart thundered with excitement as a new, untested instinct surfaced, a knowledge that was just out of reach, but *there*, where none had been before. The sudden thrill in my belly surprised me, and suddenly, terrifyingly, I heard Travis's voice inside my head, saying, *He's not crazy, Shane. He only seems crazy. He knows.*

Strangely, the locket around my neck began to feel warm, and then quite suddenly hot. I put my hand to it, and sure enough it was burning up. Even stranger than that, the tiny clasp on the heart locket had opened, something that was ordinarily difficult to do. I closed it, and tried not to panic.

Then, to my chagrin, the teacher turned his attention to me again. "Miss Clark. You're a musician. And a very good one from what I understand." His eyes were on fire with crazy delight. It scared me.

"I guess," I said, feeling creepy and uncomfortable.

"Do you have your instrument with you today?"

I shook my head. "No, sir. I'm waiting on my new one to come in. Mine was destroyed in a car crash."

"Well now, that's a shame. A crying shame. Hmm. Would you please be so kind as to bring it in when you get it, so that you could demonstrate the pentatonic scale and harmonics for the class?"

"Okay." It was odd he didn't ask about the crash, but he was weird to begin with.

"It's all part of the same thing, you know," he said, staring me down.

"Okay," I answered.

I looked over at Kelsey. Her eyes burned with amused sympathy.

Mercifully, the bell rang then, and Mr. Hedges was forced to release us to the rest of our day. Logan, in a rush to get somewhere, gave me a quick peck on the lips, and said he'd see me at lunch. It felt wrong to kiss him. Something had shifted in my heart. It didn't belong to Logan anymore. It belonged to Travis, and I had a strange sense that he was close by.

As I gathered up my books, Kelsey put a gentle hand on my arm.

"Are you sure you're okay?" she asked.

"Yeah," I lied with a fake smile. "Everything's fine."

nine

'd never lied to my mother in any significant way, so I felt like a criminal as she stood in the doorway from the laundry room to the garage the following Friday, watching me load Buddy into the Land Rover. She thought the dog and I were taking a short trip to Santa Fe, to have dinner at my dad's. I told her he and his new wife were having a big dinner party and they wanted me there. I couldn't tell her I was driving back out toward Farmington on Highway 550 to see the guy who'd saved me. I knew she was unlikely to call Dad, and he would never call her, so there was no risk in this particular fib.

I wore a pair of flattering jeans, with a couple of layered long-sleeved T-shirts, silver hoop earrings, boots, and a cute short white parka. I'd put on makeup and blown my long wavy hair out straight and shiny. I wanted to look good when Travis saw me. I thought about taking off my locket, but again it seemed to warm and glow when I thought of Travis, and something inside of me told me I needed to wear it.

"Be careful," my mother said, as she always did before I drove anywhere. "Call me if you're going to be late or if you need me for anything."

"Okay," I mumbled, unable to meet her gaze. I felt exposed and cruel, but what choice did I have? Sometimes, the truth just wasn't an option with parents.

"Have fun," my mother said. "Give your father my regards." She looked pained, and I figured this was because she still loved him. I'd heard her tell her sister once that she thought she'd always love him and never get over him, and I felt terrible for her. He was my dad, I knew that, but he wasn't worthy of my mother's love. The thought of me with him and his new wife and their baby twins was probably very difficult for her now. Poor Mom.

"Okay. Love you," I said, and I meant it, with a massive pang of guilt.

"Love you, too," she said with a sad little smile.

I climbed into the driver's seat, and closed the door. My mom kept watching me. I tried to ignore the poignant look on her face. She was sad to see me growing up. She never said it, but I sensed it. She was dreading the day I would move out and leave her all alone. I dreaded it, too, for her sake. She needed to move on from my dad, and start dating again. I didn't know how to tell her something like that, but someone needed to.

I drove for a while and as I went through the Santa Ana Indian Reservation, my heart pounded and my belly fluttered. I marveled at the stark beauty of the land as it unfolded before me. The world felt endless out here, and you could see for what seemed like hundreds of miles in every direction. You understood how small you were here, and the true force of the planet, the enormous scale of it, came over you powerfully.

Before I knew it, I was passing through the tiny town of Lybrook again. It looked the same in the sunshine as it had in the storm—small and depressing, a dry and splintered speck of civilization adrift on a sea of sand and hardened snow. I blinked, and the town was gone, already withdrawing in the rearview mirror.

I arrived at the crash site, which I now noticed was near mile marker 111, five minutes before the time I was supposed to. I parked on the north side of the highway, turned off the car, and sat for a moment, looking around expectantly. Buddy was agitated, his hackles raised. A growl rolled around in his chest. Maybe he remembered the place, and what had happened to him here. I scratched my dog behind the ears. He walked daintily onto my lap and sat down, looking up at me affectionately. I kissed his bulbous head, which smelled of dust, and lifted him up to set him on his own seat once more.

"Wait here," I said, checking my makeup and hair in the mirror. Satisfied that I looked as good as I possibly could, I exited the car, nervous with anticipation.

The air was cold and sharp, and smelled like the many ski trips I'd taken with my mother—clean, natural, outdoorsy, snowy. The scent of freedom, I thought. As before, there were no cars around. I searched for a sign of Travis, but saw nothing except the mile marker and, near it, the two small roadside crosses I'd noticed the day of my accident, stuck in the ground, one right in front of the other.

They called these types of crosses *descansos* in New Mexico, and my mother had told me that it meant "resting place" in Spanish. They weren't graves, exactly. They were informal memorials, erected in places where people had died, by those who'd loved them. Because we had a huge problem with drunk driving in our state, there were *descansos* all over the place.

Given that there was nothing much else to look at, I crossed the road to check them out, and saw that the *descansos* were made of white painted wood. I looked at the closest one. It was decorated with faded plastic flowers, a cheap teddy bear, a threadbare American flag, a Denver Broncos cup, and what appeared to be several photographs protected by plastic-zippered Baggies.

I squatted and brushed the ice and dirt from the name on the cross, and a couple of cars zipped past behind me, leaving a cold, hard wind in their wake. This reassured me a bit—should anything weird happen, there would at least be people driving on the highway today.

A name was painted onto the wood of the first cross in neat black letters, and as I read it, the ice of fear filled my veins. RANDY HARTWELL, it read. Hartwell? I recognized the last name as being the same one Travis had given me as his own. From the birth and death dates, I calculated that Randy Hartwell had been twenty-four when he died in this spot earlier this year. *On my sixteenth birthday.* Goose bumps sprouted across my arms, and crept up the back of my neck.

My eyes darted manically to the second cross, and my breath stuck in my throat. A plastic Baggie with a photograph in it covered most of the first name. Only the last two letters of the name were visible. They were *i* and *s*. My heart thundered and my belly felt sick with fear. I recognized the boy in the photograph, faded though it was. I reached out and moved the Baggie with the photo aside, and that's when I saw it. TRAVIS HARTWELL. Same death date as the other cross, different birth date. The photo in the Baggie was of the boy I knew, holding a trophy of some kind, smiling at his achievement. The news hit me like a bucket of bricks dropped upon my head. According to this *descanso*, my new friend, the beautiful boy who'd saved me, was born eighteen years ago.

And he was dead.

ten

Without realizing exactly what I was doing, I turned in a rush of terror and sprinted back to the Land Rover, overcome with fear and anxiety, fueled by instinct and adrenaline. Travis was dead?

Panic-stricken, I jumped into the driver's seat, slammed the door, and engaged the door locks. Fumbling to press the keyless ignition button, I tried to start the car, but the engine wouldn't turn over. It was completely still, and quiet. I wondered if my keys had fallen out, but realized that even so, the car would have given me the light to indicate the key was not in range. It didn't even do that. It did nothing. My panic escalated. Buddy began to whine.

Then, unfathomably, there was Travis, standing just a few feet in front of the car, wearing his jeans and his woolen jacket, boots, and hat. He smiled and waved at me as though nothing were out of the ordinary, and I felt a surge of terrified excitement. Dead or not, he was still by far the most handsome boy I had ever laid eyes on. Part of me wanted to touch him again, kiss him; the other part of me wanted to flee this place and never return.

Travis began to walk toward me, and once at the passenger-side window, he knocked on the glass for me to let him in. I stared straight ahead, nervous that if I looked into his eyes, I would weaken. He was dead, and I shouldn't be here.

"Shane!" he called out, through the window. "Are you okay?"

I shook my head.

"Shane!" he called, knocking some more and sounding worried now. "Can I please talk to you?"

"Go away!" I yelled back, still staring straight ahead. "I can't hang out with dead people!"

It sounded ridiculously stupid as I said it, and I felt bad. I sneaked a tentative look at him now. Travis cocked his head, his brow bunched up in puzzlement as he processed what I'd just told him. He shook his head, exasperated with me, glanced at the *descansos*, seemed to take a deep breath, closed his eyes for the briefest of moments, and then, to my astonishment, the passenger-door lock spontaneously disengaged. I looked about me hysterically, and frantically pressed the lock button on the door. My efforts were met with a hollow click. The master lock button didn't work anymore. I was trapped. With a dead guy.

"No!" I shrieked. "Go away! Get away from me!"

Calmly, Travis opened the passenger door and climbed in.

I tried to open my door, thinking that if he was going to be in here, then I should be out there. But it, unlike the rest of the car, it was locked. To my dismay, Buddy greeted Travis with a wagging tail, licking his hand subserviently, as though he were just the nicest and most normal person in the world.

"I can't open my door!" I shrieked.

Travis settled into the passenger seat, and shut the door behind him. I was instantly aware of the scent of warm sunshine on earth that always seemed to accompany him, and the toasty change in temperature in the car. He was like a human furnace. Or nonhuman, as the case may be. I looked at him, and instantly felt soothed and hypnotized by his incredible eyes; they radiated serenity and tranquility. The fear I'd felt began to dissolve.

"Sorry about this," he said. "I just wanted to tell you not to be afraid. It's all okay."

"What do you want from me?" I said in a hoarse whisper.

"I want you to listen to what I have to say. I don't want you to be scared, or to worry, either."

"You aren't going to eat my soul?" I asked, a bit meekly, now that I felt his peace.

Travis took a deliberate, deep breath, and blew it slowly out of his delicious-looking mouth. I should not have been noticing his perfect pink lips at a moment like this, or his brilliantly formed eyebrows and long dark eyelashes, or his exceptionally comprehending eyes, but I was under some sort of spell.

He looked directly at me and said, "Let me be clear. I. Am. Not"—he said this part haltingly and deliberately—"going to 'eat your soul.' Okay? We clear on that?"

"I saw it once on a documentary. . . ," I offered.

Travis shook his head and looked at me with pity. "You can't believe everything you see on TV. You know that. I mean, c'mon."

I looked at him for a moment, and he seemed to be telling the truth. Everything about him seemed completely genuine. His eyes, his facial expression, his body language. I was a good reader of people, usually, and there was nothing to make me think he was lying.

"So, what are you, exactly? An angel or something?" I asked.

"No, not an angel."

"Magical healer?"

94

"Nope. Not that, either."

"Then . . . what?"

"I'm dead, Shane," he said plainly. "Just like you saw on the cross. I had a bad car accident near here last year, and me and my brother died in it. I'm a revenant. Do you know what that is?"

I shook my head.

He took my hand, the electricity coming from him into my body again with exquisite pleasure, and explained calmly, "A revenant is a ghost in human form. Sometimes I'm in human form, I should say. In this dimension, during the daylight hours."

I could think of nothing to say to this. I just sat there, feeling his warmth and incredible energy. I watched him, mesmerized.

"The day we died, me and my brother did something pretty bad. Something really bad, actually."

"What did you do?" A chill shook me.

He sighed. "I don't want to talk about it right now, if that's okay with you."

I felt even more afraid. He seemed to sense this, and the energy flow from him increased, soothing me back down again before he said, "When you do something bad, and you die, one of two things happens. All of us have what's called a judgment when we die. It's decided where the soul goes next, basically. We have souls, all of us, every living thing, and they're really a form of energy. Anyway, if you've done something bad like we did, you usually end up in the Underworld when you die."

"Hell?" I asked.

"Something like that. There are lots of different names for it. We just call it the Underworld, because that's what it is."

"Who's we? You said 'we call it' that."

"Spirits. The ones I know, anyway. I don't know everything about it. I'm pretty new to this stuff, relatively."

"So is that your world, the world you told me about the other day?" My blood ran cold. "You're from hell?"

He shook his head vehemently and I was relieved. "No! Not at all. There's another option when you did something bad. If they think there's hope for your soul, you can go to the Vortex instead, and work to prove yourself, and maybe move on to the Afterworld eventually. That's my world. The Vortex."

I looked at him with confusion.

"Some people call it purgatory," he said. "It's when you did something bad, but you have good in you. You get a second chance. I'm working for that now."

"That still doesn't explain why I can touch you."

"Because I'm a revenant," he said. "As long as I'm in the Vortex I can come back here to visit, either as a revenant or as a spirit. During the day, I take human form,

96

but at night I can only visit here in spirit form. I can go back and forth pretty much whenever I want, as long as no one who knew me in life sees me when I'm a revenant."

"So, when you're not a revenant, you're like a ghost?" I asked in shock.

He grinned at my naïveté. "Not like one; I pretty much am one."

I shivered and tried to reconcile all of the fearful things I had thought about ghosts, up until then, with the kind, peaceful boy sitting here with me now.

He continued, "I have kind of like an assignment. Everyone in the Vortex gets one. I'm supposed to stick close to this road where I died, and help out, do good things for people, animals, and the land, to earn back whatever good energy I lost in the bad thing I did. It's a lot easier to help out when I'm in human form. Basically I go around all day helping rabbits that got hit by cars, things like that."

"That's why you helped me?"

He nodded. "I would have done it anyway, though."

"So basically, you haunt this road?"

"I guess you could look at it that way. I think of it more like I'm a volunteer search and rescue guy." He grinned, and looked for all the world like the most normal guy ever.

"This is hard to believe," I said.

"But you know I helped you, right?"

I nodded.

"I bet you've heard of revenants before. Around here they talk a lot about La Llorona, the woman who goes around crying on riverbanks for her dead babies. You know about her, right? She's a revenant, too. In life, she actually did kill her kids, drowned them like a crazy woman, but she had really bad postpartum depression, so they cut her some slack."

"Who are 'they'?" I asked, suddenly afraid again.

"The being or beings who make the judgments," he said. "God, the universe, whatever you want to call it. We call it the Maker of All Things. The Maker for short. Energy."

My eyes widened, and I got chills as I understood the enormity of what he'd just told me. "Have you met this being? The Maker?"

"Not directly, even though I feel him all the time. We all do, even you, if you pay attention. We're all a part of the Maker. He has helpers who tell us what's going on—I guess you'd think of them as angels in your world. Lots and lots of them. It's pretty well-organized, but not perfect. There are lots of mistakes. That's one thing I find weird. We're raised to think the Maker is perfect, but mistakes are built into every system. Can't explain it exactly. Anyway. We all have a purpose."

I sat for a moment with the knowledge that there really

98

were souls, and an afterlife, and a Maker, and angels. And a purpose. It was disconcerting, but also very comforting.

"But none of that explains how you healed me," I said after a moment. "I know I was almost dead."

Travis grinned like a little boy, adorably. "Souls in the Vortex get a bunch of cool skills to help them complete their tasks. Sometimes I feel like a superhero, like I dreamed of being when I was little. It's pretty awesome. Watch."

He pointed at the ignition button, and the car started.

"Ta-da!" he said excitedly. Then he stared at the stereo for a moment, and it turned on.

I looked at him quizzically.

He shrugged. "I don't know. Electricity. I just think about it happening, in a certain way, and it happens."

"How do you get back to the Vortex?"

"It's just dimensions, traveling between them. I know of at least four. I guess you could think of them almost as parallel universes."

"Hang on," I interrupted. "Parallel universes?"

Travis nodded. "Yeah. Worlds like this world, but in a different part of space."

"That's so weird," I said. "I have this physics teacher, Mr. Hedges. He's getting a doctorate degree in quantum physics at UNM, and all he ever talks about is parallel universes. Everyone at school thinks he's crazy. He says he found a way to access other dimensions and universes."

Travis smiled patiently. "So did I," he joked. "With a lot less school."

I smiled, but felt my heart racing. Was it a coincidence that Mr. Hedges was my teacher? I was starting to wonder if anything was a coincidence at all anymore.

"How many are there?" I asked. "Parallel universes, I mean?"

Travis shrugged. "Lots, I think. I only know about the Vortex, the Afterworld, your world, and then there's the Underworld." He seemed to shudder at the mention of this last one.

"And you've been to them all?"

"No. I can see into them, sort of, but I'm only allowed in the Vortex and your world right now."

I thought about all of this for a moment. "Was I dead when you found me?" I asked him.

He shook his head. "No way. I'm not supposed to bring people back from the dead. But if I have to, I use this."

Travis pulled a small, almost glowingly white stone from his pocket and showed it to me. "It's called a life stone, but no one uses it. At least no one I know in the Vortex, because you don't stay in the Vortex if you use it. Bringing a soul back means the Maker has to reset the clockwork of the universe, basically. It has severe consequences."

"Why would they even give you that rock if you're not supposed to use it?"

Travis looked at the stone thoughtfully. "Best I figure is it's some kind of a test. The Maker's real big on tests. We get tested a lot, on your side and on mine, and a lot of us, I'm sorry to say, fail. I've met souls in the Vortex who just disappear one day, because they failed a test. One idiot tried to use the life stone to bring himself back from the dead. Never heard from him again."

"Would I have died if you hadn't found me?"

"I'm no doctor, but I'd say probably so."

"So you did save my life."

He looked into my eyes with a small nod, and seemed quite modest, considering.

"How did you find me, anyway?" I asked.

"I get a sense of things, and I go where I'm needed," he said. "I have different ways of moving through time and space than you do."

"Well, however you did it, thank you. I should have said that before."

Tears welled in my eyes as I considered how suspicious I'd been of him earlier, how afraid I'd been, when he was heroic and kind and had saved me. Seeing my tears, he reached out across the center console to hug me, and my locket warmed on my chest at his touch. I felt completely and entirely at home in his arms; that was the only way I could describe it. I buried my face in his warm, solid chest, and breathed in his scent of sunshine and earth. I didn't want to let go, but he pulled back after a while. When we came out of the incredible, intoxicating embrace, I had a driving need to kiss him; it was more urgent than anything else in my life ever had been. It was overpowering. I looked at his lips, and moved closer, pulled by a force larger than myself directly toward him. Travis looked at me like he wanted to kiss me, too, but pulled away suddenly, almost angrily.

"Don't," he said.

It hurt my feelings terribly.

"Why not?"

"Rules," he sighed. He looked as frustrated as I was. "I want to, Shane. Trust me, I do. But I'm not supposed to have any kind of intimate contact with a living human in your world while I'm in revenant form. It's strictly forbidden."

"But we've been holding hands, and hugging. That's intimate."

"I'm pretty sure by *intimate* they mean kissing, and all that other stuff. You know. Exchanging fluids. That's what they mean."

I made a gross-out face at his terminology, and he laughed.

"To be blunt, I guess they don't want living people having babies with revenants."

"You can still . . . do that?" I asked, my curiosity over-riding any discomfort I might have had with discussing the biological function in question.

"Absolutely. I'm in human form, that means everything about me works, just like a real man, while I'm here."

I felt my belly flutter to think of him "working like a real man," and this embarrassed me.

"So," he said, sensing my discomfort and changing the subject. "That's the reasoning, anyway. It just isn't allowed."

"Well, it's not like I want to die and have your baby like in some vampire movie. I just wanted to kiss you."

He answered by smiling playfully at me, in a way that gave me a pleasant rush. I brushed against his arm. Again, the flood of energy, a mild and pleasant buzzing sensation, filled me.

"Travis," I said, touching his arm and igniting the cur-rent again. "Do you feel that? Like a shock, but a good shock? Like a flood of light under your skin? Whenever we touch, I feel like I get shocked, but in a good way."

He watched me coolly, a sexy sort of intelligence and wisdom radiating from his eyes. "Heck yeah, I feel it. Feels really good. Better than almost anything."

He put his hand over mine and squeezed it. Those beautiful eyes and long, dark eyelashes of his broke my heart somehow. How could someone so young and beautiful be dead? It wasn't right.

He laced his fingers through mine, and I could feel our energy mingling, surging through the rest of my body. He then unlaced our fingers and ran his fingertips lightly across my palm. It was exquisite, the way his touch made me feel, and exciting in a very grown-up, very secret, womanly kind of way. When he looked at me again, his eyes were filled with a powerful longing that I am fairly certain was mirrored in my own gaze.

He spoke in a soft voice. "This is why I had to see you again." He squeezed my hand and a delicious heat coursed through me, to places no boy had ever touched before. "This." He closed his eyes, reveling in the sensation. "I've helped a few other people, and lots of animals, but I never felt anything like what I feel with you."

I tried to comprehend what he was saying.

"We're not really even doing anything, right? Just holding hands, but man. It's . . . so good."

"Just one kiss?" I asked, almost begged.

He stroked my cheek with his hand, and looked longingly into my eyes, but shook his head decidedly no.

"Absolutely not. But you know, and I shouldn't probably even tell you this, but there's one exception to the intimacy rule."

I perked up. "Oh?"

"It's very rare, though. It pretty much never happens.

Nobody I know in the Vortex ever heard of it actually happening." He paused, and gave me a significant look. "It's when a revenant finds his Kindred in another dimension. Then the cross-dimensional laws don't apply."

"His what?"

"Kindred. You know, like kindred spirits? There's actually a way to measure that stuff, I guess. It has to do with vibrations. Souls vibrate at frequencies, just like musical notes or radio waves. When they vibrate in harmonic unison, that's a Kindred."

"This is just like what Mr. Hedges talks about all the time!"

"Yeah?"

"The golden ratio, and the Fibonacci series. How music and chemistry and geometry are all the same thing expressed in different ways."

Travis looked confused. "I don't know about all that," he said, "but I do know that Kindreds are the only ones who can . . . you know."

"Hook up?"

He looked at me hungrily. "Yeah. Cross-dimensionally."

"But it's never happened?" I asked.

"Oh, it's happened. Just not to anyone I know. They say some of the world's top prophets and spiritual leaders were born from unions between Kindreds in different dimensions."

"How do we find out if we're Kindreds?" I asked, excited by this possibility.

"I don't know," he said with a furrowed brow, as though deeply bothered by this. "But I want to find out. I honestly didn't think much about it until I met you. When I touched you, and felt the intense energy between us, I know this sounds weird, but I feel like we might be—you know, Kindreds."

"Can we just kiss and find out?" I said, moving in again.

"No," he said firmly, pushing me away. "It's not a chance either of us wants to take. Trust me. If we do, we could both end up somewhere we don't want to be."

"So I'll never be able to kiss you?" I asked, despondent.

"I don't know," he said sadly. "I'll ask around in the Vortex to see if there's a way for us to find out. But you know, just holding your hand is better than any kiss I ever had before. I mean that."

I nodded weakly. "Yeah, but if it feels this good to hold hands, just imagine."

He blinked slowly, as though he was much more mature than I was, and frustrated by me. "I'm sorry. I just—you have to understand that I have to be really careful about these things right now. There's a lot at stake."

"Your soul."

Travis nodded and his eyes scanned the horizon. "It's getting late," he said. "Thanks for coming all the way out

106

here. I wanted to show you my 'haunt,' and explain it all to you here, where nobody else could hear us, in case you freaked out—which you did." He smiled affectionately at me. "You should get home. The sun will be going down soon. I have to get back to the Vortex."

"How do you get there?" I asked, fascinated.

He hesitated as if trying to decide whether to tell me the truth or not. "There are portals all over the world, energy centers for the planet. One of them is here, near Chaco Canyon. I use that one usually, but supposedly I can use any of them."

"Can I go with you?" I asked, excited by the idea of seeing the Vortex.

"No. You don't belong there. You should get on home."

He opened his door and stepped out, all business now. "I'll find you again soon. I promise. Be careful."

I watched as he jogged across the road, and then off into the desert. It was devastating to watch him leave. I knew he'd told me to go home, but I also knew that, for better or worse, I seemed to be suddenly turning into a girl who didn't necessarily do what people told her to anymore.

When he'd gotten a good distance away, I started the Land Rover, and used it for what it was designed for, going off-road and into the desert, to follow him.

eleven

I trailed Travis across the empty, frozen desert for what felt like more than an hour. Travis seemed to be starting to sense something, and every so often spun to look back in my direction. I slowly braked the car until he continued on, quick and graceful as a deer—or as a revenant, I suppose.

The terrain got rougher the farther we got from the road, more craggy, with rocky hills popping up, and then growing into ever larger mesas and flat-topped rock formations. I began to realize how stupid I was. It was nearly dark now, and I had no idea how to get back, much less how to change a tire if I blew one out here. It seemed there was no turning around now, so I drove as far as I could, but eventually parked behind a tall crag, kissed Buddy, and peeked out to see where Travis had gone. I saw the vast stone and mud-brick ruins of Chaco Canyon, remnants of a large and thriving Native American city that had occupied this spot more than a thousand years ago.

Travis came to a stop just past the ruins, against the sheer wall of the canyon, and scaled the rock face like Spider-Man, using carved footholds in the wall. It was effortless for him, and in a matter of minutes he'd climbed maybe three stories or so, and disappeared into what appeared to be the opening of a large cave.

I waited a couple of seconds, then hurried to the same spot at the canyon wall. I had taken rock-climbing lessons for years with my mom, at the indoor climbing gym in Albuquerque, and knew more or less what I was doing—though I'd never done it outdoors or without being tethered and belayed by a competent adult. I was relieved that the holds were solid, and deep, and I felt confident that I could make it. Adrenaline pumping, I began to climb up after him. My breath came fast from exertion. Halfway up, a droning sensation in my spine, a sixth sense, hummed, pulsed, and chilled me to the bone. Nonetheless, I continued up, and at last climbed through the small entrance, into a tight and narrow corridor that burrowed down at a steep angle, deep into the canyon. I crouched through the slippery corridor and into an enormous cave that seemed to open into three other caves of equal or greater size. I should not have been able to see here, but the walls seemed to glow with a faint yellowish light, and I saw the shadows of people seemingly walking inside the walls of the cave. I started. These people weren't walking, they were floating. And they were coming into the cavern through its walls. My instincts told me to run, but something kept me there—my need to find Travis.

The cavern was a maze of stalactites and stalagmites, some big enough to hide me. I ducked behind the nearest stalagmite, hoping to avoid being seen by any of the beings here. I heard voices murmuring, and realized I could not understand the languages. So many of them were being spoken, all at once. What were these things? Were they also ghosts, or revenants?

I peeked out, and looked for Travis in the crowd. I spotted him off by himself, sort of kneeling near the back wall as though he were in church, in front of the opening to one of the caves. Next to him, a large pool of water on the floor was fed by an occasional drip from the ceiling of the cave. I tiptoed to the next closest stalagmite, and hid again, peeking out to see what Travis was doing, trying to avoid being seen. I watched in astonishment as the center doorway began to glow, throwing a warm orange light out onto Travis. A low humming filled the cavern, a pitch that resonated within me in a very pleasant way.

Travis stood now and held his arms to his sides. I was

so astonished by what I saw that I did not even notice the young man approaching from the dark to my right, until he was right upon me and speaking into my ear, his breath redolent of beer and cigarette smoke.

"Well, hello there," the male voice said.

I gasped and jumped, startled. I spun to look at him and saw a handsome man perhaps a few years older than Travis, familiar to me from the photos on the other *descanso.*

"Randy?" I asked, incredulous. He and Travis were the only figures in the cave that looked like regular, solid living people, like me. Everyone else looked like a shadow or a ghost.

He was surprised. "Have we met?" he asked. "I thought you were new here."

Frightened that Travis would see me, and not knowing what to do, I ducked out of sight and put my finger to my lips to indicate that Randy should be quiet. He seemed to find this very amusing, in the way only drunk people can find things amusing. He followed the line of where my eyes had been looking, and laughed loudly, coldly.

"Are you afraid of my brother?" he asked. "Mr. Goody Two-shoes over there?"

"Please, don't bring attention to me," I pleaded in a whisper. "I'm not supposed to be here."

Randy tipped a flask into his mouth, and took a drag from a cigarette, observing me with half-closed eyes.

"Yeah, well, I'm not supposed to bring whiskey in here from out there either, but I do it. Sometimes rules were meant to be broken, right, babe?"

He seemed quite drunk already.

"Hey, Travis!" he shouted across the cavern, to my horror. "Get your ass over here! I think you should see this!"

Suddenly Travis's chanting and the low drone sound stopped. I peeked out and saw the orange glow in the small cave opening sputter out. Travis spun around, facing the exact stalagmite where I hid.

"Who's up there?" he called. "Randy?"

"A pretty new girl who's afraid you'll see her watching you," Randy called. Looking at me now he asked, "So, tell me, how'd you bite it?"

"Bite what?" I asked, disgusted by him.

Randy laughed. "Die, darlin'. How'd you die?"

"I, what?" I asked, confused. "I didn't die. I'm not— I'm alive. I'm not one of you."

Randy's expression went from flirty to stupefied. "You're what, now?" he asked, as though he might not have heard me right.

I said nothing, because I could hear Travis coming toward us at a run. I felt my breath catch in my throat. In an instant, Travis was upon us, standing between me and Randy with a simmering fury in his eyes. Travis shoved Randy away and pulled me to the side.

"Shane! What are you doing here?" Travis asked, aghast.

"I wanted to see where you go," I said meekly. I smiled sweetly and hoped he wouldn't stay mad at me.

"There are rules," he hissed. "I told you not to come here. It's a place for the dead. Not for you. How did you even get here?"

"I just followed you."

Travis looked out at the darkening sky, concerned. He took a deep breath to compose himself, and told me, "Listen. I know you don't mean any harm. But we have to get back now. We check in each sundown. I'm not supposed to still be on this side like this, but I can't leave you out here with Victor out there."

"Victor's not *my* enemy," I said. "I can just find my way back."

"Yes, he *is* your enemy. He's trying to harm you."

"I don't understand."

Travis stared me down, hard, as though I were very stupid and had missed some crucial detail. "The day you crashed," he said. "What happened before I got there, exactly?"

I told him quickly about the coyote in the road.

"That was Victor," he explained.

"Victor's a coyote?" I asked.

"No. Victor's an incubus."

"A what?"

"A demon from the first level of the Underworld. A shape-shifter," he explained hurriedly. "He knew me in life, and he comes to your world with only a couple of goals in mind: to kill people for fun, and to try to ruin my and Randy's chances of getting to the Afterworld. Sometimes he's a coyote. He can be almost anything he wants, whenever he wants."

I froze in fear.

Travis thought for a moment, and said, "Wait here for me. Stay quiet, and don't move. I'll go check into the Vortex, and then I'll return, but not like this. When I come back, I'll be nothing but energy and maybe faint wisps of light that will look like smoke or shadows to you."

"A ghost?" I whispered.

He nodded, and I felt guilty for causing all of this.

"I'm sorry."

"It's okay. We'll get you back to your car. Wait here. It'll be maybe fifteen minutes, okay?"

"Okay." I hesitated, watching behind him as the stream of people-things continued to enter the cavern. "What are all of those?"

"Spirits," he said.

"Do they know I'm here?" I asked.

"Some probably do, most probably don't. They leave their dimensions for their own purposes, and return to their own times. The ones you can see pretty well, solid like me and Randy, are from our time. The see-through ones are from another time. Dusk is when we all have to return to change form."

I shivered, and watched. "Does that mean that maybe some of the people I've thought were regular people in my everyday life might have been something else?"

He smiled. "We're still people," he said. "We're just in a different energy form."

"You know what I mean."

"Yes. Probably. I don't really know, Shane. My haunting area is pretty remote. I don't do a lot of socializing in any of the dimensions. I gotta go. I'll be back in a while. You'll be okay."

"I'm afraid."

"Don't be. But to be safe, you should stay behind this thing," he said, indicating the stalagmite.

"How will I know when you're back here, if I can't see you?" I asked in a panic.

"You'll have to feel me, and focus on that. I'll try to make it clear where I am. I'll lead you back to your car and I'll protect you from Victor. If he senses you mean something to me, he'll go out of his way to hurt you."

"Oh my God," I said, terrified now.

"Just wait here, touch nothing. Got it? Can you do that?"

I hung my head and nodded. When I looked up, I saw his body had begun to fade, as though it were in a darker space than mine. I gasped.

"It's happening," he said, observing his hand as it seemed to turn, for a moment, into a swarm of miniscule fireflies. "The sun's just about down. Wait for me here. I don't have much time."

I stared at him as his body seemed to dissolve, melting away like honey in a cup of hot tea, into the air around us. It finally sank in, in that moment, that he wasn't like me.

The portal began to glow in the distance again, and again came the low hum. I watched with tremendous sadness as Travis's body evaporated into a trail of vapor, and was sucked into the portal like water down a drain.

Once he'd gone, the portal returned to its darkened state until the next revenant took her place before it, began to chant and transmutate, and was gone. There was a line of them, all going into the Vortex. I watched in utter amazement. Randy was at the end of the line, drinking and smoking, and unlike the others, he stopped before the third portal, and reached a hand out to touch it. A thread of what looked like dark, wispy electricity came out and shocked him, quite badly from what I could see, and he backed away. He began to dissolve. And then, as the others were quickly sucked away to the Vortex, Randy, too, was pulled in. Before long, every spirit was gone with the last flicker of the sun.

Suddenly, I was alone. The cave walls stopped glowing. The drone ceased. The darkness and the cold enveloped me completely, and I began to tremble head to toe, thinking of Victor and how he'd tried to kill me once already. I remembered the demonic thing outside the guest bedroom the night of the accident. Had that, too, been Victor? Was he following me?

I took my cell phone from the pocket of my jacket, and checked to see if I got reception out here, in case of an emergency. There were no bars at all. Nothing but the red SOS notice that indicated no service. This was why it was all that much more mysterious and frightening that at that exact instant, the phone rang, with the song I'd programmed in for my mother. My mom was calling me? But how? It should have been impossible, given the lack of reception here.

I answered the call, whispering because Travis had told me not to make any noise.

"Hello?" I said. "Mom? Is that you? Can you hear me?"

I heard wet-sounding heavy breathing, low like a man's, and in the background the blare of loud Western music, and the staccato of people arguing. It sounded like a bar or something. I couldn't imagine my mother, the classical music fan who never went on dates, being in an environment like that.

"Hello?" I asked again, my pulse beating faster. "Mom?"

"Well, hello there," growled an unclean-sounding, very low, very rough man's voice. A sudden chill of fear swept through me. I felt the lewd, greasy presence of the voice through the phone, and dirty fingers of anxiety crawled up and down my skin.

"I'm sorry," I choked out lamely. "You must have the wrong number."

"No," said the voice seductively. "You're Shane Clark. I want to talk to you." I heard his Western accent now, thick and heavy. "How are you liking the cave of the damned?" The question terrified me. I began to look around frantically, horrified.

"Who *is* this?" I asked, my voice breaking with nerves.

He answered me with a vulgar laugh.

"Randy?" I asked.

"No, not Randy."

"Who is this?" I asked.

"Listen," he oozed. "I have a message for yer boyfriend. You tell him I'm gonna git you. You tell him I don't fail."

I couldn't answer. I was petrified, sickened, horrified. This made him laugh again.

"You give him that message for me. Okay, baby?"

He made a disgusting sound, as though he were a dog licking its chops, and his breathing got faster and louder, punctuated with grunting. When I failed to answer him, he groaned in a filthy, nauseating way.

"You tell him something else for me. Tell him that if he wants to find your little fleabag, he knows where to look."

The man let out a blood-freezing howl that seemed to come from the pits of hell itself. A coyote howl. Then he began to laugh, hideously, obscenely. My mind raced to Buddy. That was the only little fleabag I could think of, and I'd left him all alone in the Land Rover.

In a sick panic, I pressed the buttons on the phone, trying to end the call. Nothing worked. I scrambled to remove the back cover, and pried the battery out. The phone went dead. I curled up against a wall in the darkness. Outside a coyote greeted the night with a long and dissonant wail.

twelve

Minutes later, as I sat on the floor of the cave, rocking and hugging my knees, scarcely daring to breathe, silently praying and begging for Travis to return, I saw a faint glimmer of lights in my peripheral vision. Frightened, I snapped my head toward the lights, and where they had been I now saw a faint smoky shape floating in the air, sort of pale blue, about the size of a man.

"Travis?" I called softly, my heart hammering in my chest. What if it wasn't him? What if it was whoever had just called me? The smoke undulated a bit, and sort of snaked along in the air toward me. Instinctively, I scooted away from it, until my back was pressed hard against the uneven surface of the cavern wall. I trembled. The haze seemed to pause, and it began to fade away. It was almost worse not to see it, because I knew it was still there, just invisible now.

"Travis?" I whispered. "Please don't leave me here alone. Please give me some sign that it's you."

A brighter light caught my attention now, near the ceiling of the cave. I looked up and saw an orb, made of faint blue light, hovering above me. It hummed, in harmonic intervals of sound. I powerfully sensed his presence, in a way that is almost impossible to describe. I just knew, much as I had known he was with me in the dream. I felt his energy, and his smile, and his calm confidence as it surrounded me protectively. I knew that everything was going to be okay.

"I feel you," I whispered. "I know you're here."

The orb moved now, first drifting down to eye level in front of me, and then zipping with incredible speed across the cave and back, leaving a trail of soft, shimmering light in its wake, like the faintest of tiny comets. It stopped, and hovered, until the light trails had disappeared, and then began to move again, this time tracing the shape of a heart in the air, with a smiley face in the middle. The fear drained out of me.

"You're silly," I whispered, and told him about the phone call. As I spoke, the orb glowed brighter, as if to reassure me he could still protect me.

The orb floated to the lip of the cave now, and went

down, then back up toward me. It reminded me of the way a dog will run to you and then away and then back to you when it wants to be followed. Travis wanted me to go down the rock wall. Gingerly, I let myself over the edge, and felt with my toes for the indentions in the rock. I wished I had a rope to tether me to the wall. It was never smart to climb without one, especially in the dark, but a full moon had risen and there was enough light for me to see. Slowly, I descended, all the while with Travis hovering just beside me, reassuringly.

When I touched the ground, I heard the coyote howl, answered by others yipping madly. I began to shake, and the orb expanded into smoke again, and enveloped me for a moment. It was an invisible embrace that filled me with peace, calm, and strength. Travis. His spirit was so soothing to me, so profoundly peaceful, I could not imagine what he might have done to deserve the Vortex. I knew he was trying to protect me. I also knew, in that same unspoken way, that whoever had called me was out there, watching us, waiting.

Travis took on the orb shape again and zoomed along the path a few yards, then hovered to wait for me to follow. I traipsed clumsily along after him, trying not to notice the eerie night calls coming from the distance.

I could see light streaming from behind the crag where I had parked my car. As we rounded the rock, I saw that the headlights were on and every door was open, pouring yellow light from the interior of the car into the black night in every direction.

"Buddy!" I cried, starting for the car. Quickly, the orb was in front of me, glowing powerfully in a pulsating rhythm, as though in warning. I understood instantly. Be cautious. I slowed to a walk again, worried about my sweet little dog.

As we drew closer to my car, the orb became vapor, and enveloped me again, protectively. The peace it had given me earlier was weakened now, though; I didn't know if this was because I was fretting so much over my dog or because Travis was also worried. I wished I could ask him and get an answer.

Soon enough, I saw that the car was empty. Buddy was gone. "No!"

The vapor undulated a moment, then became an orb again, darting into the vehicle as though checking it out for safety. I knew I was to wait until he was done with this inspection. I remembered the phone call, how the caller had told me to tell Travis that he'd know where to find my friend. Victor had my dog.

"Travis," I called out to the orb. "It's him. Victor took Buddy. He warned me about it when he called my cell phone. He said you'd know where to find him."

The orb continued its check of the car, under the seats,

around the steering wheel, under the car itself, on top as well. Then, in a display of what I could only think was poltergeist power, Travis somehow closed all the doors except for the driver's side one. The orb, growing paler— perhaps from exertion—came to a halt directly in front of me.

And then my phone vibrated with a text message. I looked at the caller ID, and it was the line of continuous zeros I'd gotten when Travis had phoned me at the hospital.

The text read: GO HOME NOW.

The orb floated into the car and hovered over the steering wheel, an invitation for me to go.

"Okay," I said, shaking. "But I can't just leave Buddy out there all alone!"

The orb stayed put, and I could almost see Travis sighing in frustration with me. I sensed that he was very tired.

In the near distance, again I heard a coyote howl, and I hurtled my body into the car and slammed the door behind me. The locks engaged without me doing anything, Travis protecting me yet again. The orb began to fade before my eyes, thinning to vapor, curling slowly into the darkness.

"I guess this is good night," I said. "Thank you. Please help me find Buddy."

The smoke enveloped me, and I did my best to hug back, mentally. Slowly, the smoke faded to nothingness, and I assumed this meant Travis had returned to wherever he needed to go. I looked out at the night, and saw a pair of glowing red eyes staring down at me from the rise. The eyes looked happy. Laughing. I hated them, and whomever they belonged to. I began to cry for Buddy, imagining the worst. I started the engine, revved it a couple of times in fury toward Victor—I was almost completely certain this was all his fault—before pulling a tight, fast U-turn.

Mercifully, Travis's orb guided me until I hit the smooth blacktop of the highway. I hated leaving Buddy out there! But I comforted myself with the thought that Travis was looking for him. He knew how much I loved that dog. Victor must have been counting on that.

I leaned forward over the steering wheel as though that might somehow make me go faster. I fumbled for the phone pieces in my pocket with one hand, and as I drove managed to put the thing back together again.

Instinctively, I called Kelsey, using the car's wireless device so that I could keep both hands on the wheel. Her voice was cheerful and normal coming through the car's speakers, and I told her everything. I released all the tension and fear, and sobbed, and she reassured me and asked me to take a deep breath, to slow down, to tell her again so she understood.

"Where are you now?" she finally asked when I'd finished.

"Coming home, driving."

"Please be careful," she said.

"I am."

"I'm worried about you."

"Me, too," I said, staring out at the cold, dark night.

"Call me when you get home to let me know you're okay," she said.

We ended the call after that, and whatever small reassurance had come from hearing my best friend's voice was replaced almost immediately by a silent, ominous dread. I remembered my mother's words, about how there were no atheists in an emergency. I finally understood what she'd meant. I began to mutter a prayer to the Maker under my breath—for Buddy, but also for Travis, and for myself, and for all the world, really, because for the first time in my life I knew, really knew, that evil existed, and that sometimes, in spite of us being good people, it had the power to reach out and snatch from us the things we loved the most.

thirteen

By the time I made it to the comforting urban lights and sprawl of Albuquerque, I couldn't see any sign of Travis still with me. No sign of Victor, either. I was about to turn into the long curving driveway to my house when I saw Kelsey's red Prius parked at the curb out front. It took me all of two seconds to figure out that it had been a colossal mistake to tell her everything about Travis and the Vortex, the eerie phone call and my kidnapped dog. She'd told my mother.

I let myself in through the garage, and tiptoed into the house.

My mother and Kelsey sat side by side at the granite island in the kitchen, facing the laundry room, waiting for me. Kelsey had a bottle of fancy Italian pear soda, the kind my mom got from Whole Foods, while my mother, in her nightgown, appeared to have consumed an entire bottle of red wine—a sure sign that she was not happy, and that I was in big trouble. The last two times my mother had waited up for me with a bottle of wine, I'd been grounded for two weeks.

"Hi," I said miserably, dropping my keys into the wicker basket on the counter.

"Oh, Shane," my mother groaned. She shook her head, disappointed and concerned, but also relieved that I had made it home. I hated that particular combination of parental mixed emotions.

I blinked obnoxiously at my former best friend, feeling incredibly naked and betrayed. "Well, hello, Kelsey," I said facetiously. "What a surprise to find you here at eleven thirty at night on a Friday."

"I told you, I was worried about you," Kelsey said, her face registering terrible hurt. She thought she was helping me. Of course she did. Never tell the daughter of psychotherapists you're visiting a hot dead guy in a cave, or that you get calls from scary people on dead phones, or that your dog has been taken by a demon named Victor.

Lesson learned.

"So, is that what the party's for?" I asked sarcastically, indicating the wine bottle. "Shane's gone cuh-ray-zay, let's whoop it up?"

I was angry. I'd been through too much that day. I just wanted to drop into my bed and sleep.

"Kelsey called me after you called her from Chaco Canyon tonight," my mother told me, standing up and coming to put her hands on my shoulders while she searched my eyes, her own filled with deep sorrow and grave concern. I hated this look.

"Great," I said, averting my gaze.

"Shane, we need to talk." My mother ducked down, trying to reconnect her bloodshot gaze with mine, but I turned away.

"No, we don't," I said, shrugging out of her grasp. I stormed from the room.

"Get back here, young lady!"

"Just leave me alone!" I yelled back.

I heard feet running down the hall after me, and Kelsey and my mother tag-teamed me, grabbing me and dragging me back to the great room, forcing me onto the sofa. They looked so self-righteous it made me want to throw up. They had no idea what I'd been through, and there was no way I could tell them and have them believe me. Holding me down on the sofa, and kneeling at my feet, my mother said sternly, "Shane Clark, where is your dog?"

I said nothing.

"Did you take Buddy out into the desert and lose

him?" my mother asked me, mortified.

"I didn't lose him. He was taken."

"Oh, my Lord," said my mother. "Who took him?"

I stared stonily ahead and said nothing.

My mother continued the interrogation. "Did you actually tell Kelsey you were rescued by a dead boy? And that you tried to go to purgatory to visit him? Did you lose your poor dog in the middle of the freezing desert?"

I refused to look at either one of them.

My mother sighed unhappily.

Kelsey rubbed my arm. "Tell your mom what you told me about your ghost friend and the demon, and how he stole Buddy to bait the ghost so he could ruin his chances at going to heaven."

"The Afterworld," I corrected instinctively, then flinched with regret.

Kelsey and my mother exchanged a look of bewilderment.

"Oh, my God," said my mother, but not because she was worried Victor might get to me. She was upset that I was insane. "What is happening to you, Shane? This isn't like you at all!"

"I'd like to go to bed now," I said.

"Shane, honey. Listen to me. I'm a doctor. What you're saying, it's not normal. Surely you can understand that."

"I realize that," I told her, finally making eye contact. "You think I don't realize that? I don't want this to be happening to me! It wasn't my choice. I don't understand it, either. And I'm not lying. I'm not making this up."

"I know, honey." I could tell from the look on my mother's face that she thought she had made some sort of breakthrough with me. "Listen to me. It's not unusual to have hallucinations after hitting your head really hard. If you've injured your occipital lobes, it can lead to hallucinations." She put her hand on the back of my head. "That's here, sweetie."

"I didn't hit my head!"

"That's not what you told me," Kelsey said guiltily. She did not enjoy betraying me, I could tell, but she felt it was her duty. She looked at my mother again and spoke of me as if I weren't there. "She told me she was nearly dead and that this ghost cowboy dude rescued her with stones and a slingshot before a gang of coyotes ate her."

I gulped and said nothing. The looks on their faces were so insulting, and yet I understood it completely. If the situation had been reversed, if Kelsey had been the one in the accident, who met the ghost, and she had called me two weeks ago or so to tell me about it, I would have thought she was nuts, too.

"I know it sounds weird, okay?" I said impatiently. "But these things really did happen to me. If you love me, you have to believe me!"

"Shane," my mother said again, in a patronizing tone. "Tell me, have you had trouble recognizing colors at all? Has it been harder to read and write since the crash? Have you noticed that it's harder for you to recognize or understand things that are drawn on paper?"

"No! I'm fine. I swear! I had tests done, you saw the results yourself."

"Sometimes tests miss things." My mother looked at me as though I were a pitiful orphan rather than her own child. "Have you had trouble reading music? Or have you had any blind spots in your field of vision?"

"No, Mom! Stop examining me! I'm not your patient!"

Kelsey and my mother exchanged a look of sadness.

"It's not unusual, Shane, to hit the back of your head in a car crash. The seat back is right there. Car crashes are common causes of this type of trauma."

"I'm fine. I don't have any trauma."

This went on for a time, my mother playing doctor and Kelsey biting her lower lip and staring at the floor, while I tried to figure out a way to make this all better. I couldn't. There was no way. They were convinced I was losing my mind.

Once the interrogation was over and my mother had announced that I would need to be taken to a brain trauma specialist, and Kelsey had apologized and told me that she had only done this for my own good, I asked if I could eat something. I was suddenly starving. My mother said yes, and she and Kelsey followed me to the kitchen, watching over me like hawks.

I poured myself a large bowl of cereal and milk. I took this to the living room, trailed by both of them as surely as a mental patient might be trailed by orderlies with clipboards. I sat in the chair across the coffee table from the sofa, and they sat anxiously on the sofa to watch me. My mother looked me up and down with worry. I looked her up and down with what I hoped was a blank expression. I resisted throwing cereal at her.

"We're going to help you get through this, sweetie," she told me uncertainly.

I spooned cereal into my mouth and said nothing, chewing with my mouth open because I knew it would annoy her.

"Is there anything else you want to tell me about what you've been seeing and experiencing?" my mother asked.

"Considering that I never wanted to tell you any of it at all, no," I replied. "Oh, wait. Yes, there is something. Kelsey met him. The 'imaginary' cowboy who rescued me. She thought he was hot, too. Did she tell you that part?"

My mother, shocked and suddenly suspicious, looked at Kelsey for an answer. "No, she didn't," she said.

"You saw him, right?" I asked Kelsey. "But now you're acting like it's all made up."

"I saw a guy, yes, and he was dressed like a cowboy," Kelsey said. "He had her necklace," Kelsey explained. "He said he found it at the crash site, but I bet he stole it so he'd have a reason to find her again. He brought it back to her at the bagel shop. He obviously isn't a ghost. Just some random guy."

"He's not just some guy," I insisted, tears burning in my eyes and spilling down my cheeks. "He's—he's perfect. I love him."

Kelsey hugged her chest and looked around, making me think at least some small part of her believed me. My mother was not buying any of it, however. She was starting to cry with frustration and anxiety.

"This is worse than I thought," she said. "But we'll help you, darling. We will. I promise you that."

"You know what, you guys?" I said before slurping down the last of the milk from my bowl. "I am just really, really tired. And I'd like to be alone now."

"That's a sign of brain trauma," my mother assured me.

"It's also a sign of it being night and me being human. So if you're done telling me I'm psychotic, I'd like to go to bed."

"No one's saying you're psychotic," my mother said,

insulted. "What you likely have is trauma, to your occipital lobe and possibly other parts of the brain. It's perfectly normal to go through what you're going through, honey. I know that's hard to believe right now, but I am begging you, as your mother here, and not wearing my doctor hat, as your mother I am begging you, whatever rational bit of my amazing daughter we have left fighting in that beautiful brain of yours, I am begging you to at least consider the possibility that everything you think is happening might not actually be happening. Okay? Can we at least do that?"

I held the empty bowl in my lap and looked at it, and wondered if there was any way she could be right. If I'd only hit my head, like she said, then I might have imagined the injuries, and then imagined them going away. I might have imagined all of it. I might have just been sitting in the Land Rover the whole time today, dreaming that I was going into the Vortex. I shivered at this new possibility. What if she was right?

"Okay," I said, starting to doubt myself in a very disturbing way. "Can we agree to say none of us know what's happening to me, until I see the brain doctor? And will you leave me alone until then?"

"Sure, honey. As long as you don't go driving around. In fact, I don't want you driving anywhere until this is resolved." My mother's face brightened for the first time since I'd come home, and she got up to hug me. "I'm proud of you. It takes a strong girl to admit she might be hallucinating."

"Yes, I think I saw that on a poster in the counseling office," I said. "Very inspiring, Mom."

My mother laughed, and kissed me softly on the head. "Nice to see you still have your sense of humor. That bodes well for your recovery."

"If I'm sick," I corrected her.

"If you're sick," she said condescendingly.

"I'm sorry, Shane," Kelsey told me, getting up to hug me, too. She had tears in her eyes, but I didn't return her embrace. "I know you're mad at me, but I think someday you'll thank me. I did it because I love you."

I said nothing in return.

"I really hope you're still going to help me with the Christmas party next weekend," Kelsey told me.

"Sure," I said.

"We should let her rest," my mother told Kelsey.

"Okay," Kelsey said. "Good-bye, Dr. Romero. Bye, Shane."

My mother hugged Kelsey tightly and thanked her. "My daughter doesn't know how lucky she is to have a friend like you," she said. "Tell your parents they raised a great kid, okay?"

"Okay," Kelsey said with a self-conscious giggle. "Bye."

And with that sickening display of affection mercifully ended, I plunked my dirty bowl into the sink, and staggered off down the hall to my room, locking the door behind me.

I went to the computer on my desk, and moved the mouse to wake it. Then I opened the internet browser, and went to the search engine. I typed in "Travis Hartwell" and "New Mexico," pressed Enter, and waited. Moments later it returned a page of results, the top six of which were stories from the *Valencia County Times* about rodeo competitions. I scanned past these, looking for something else—and found it.

The seventh entry was a news brief from an Albuquerque television station. The headline confirmed my worst fears, and also confirmed that my mother was wrong about me: BELOVED BELEN BROTHERS DEAD IN FIERY CRASH.

I clicked on the story. It told of a freak accident on Highway 550, in which a truck hauling a horse drove off a cliff and was instantly incinerated. The truck belonged to a ranch owner named Deirdre Hartwell of Belen, New Mexico, but was mostly used by her younger son, a rodeo competitor. The boy and the horse were killed in the crash.

Suddenly, the pendant on my neck felt hot. I put my hand to it and nearly burned myself. Unable to bear its heat against my skin, I quickly undid the clasp and dropped the pendant on the desk. It seemed to be throbbing with light for a moment, and then cooled down. I was on the right track.

I continued to read the news story.

The truck was driven by her two sons, Travis and Randy Hartwell, last seen at a rodeo competition where Travis, a straight-A student at Belen High, had placed first in calf roping. Randy, a part-time student at the University of New Mexico, was employed at his mother's ranch and often supported his brother during competitions. Hartwell was surprised to learn that her sons had been so far from home and had no explanation for why they might have been driving on that isolated road. The heartbroken Hartwell, who had only these two children, said that they were "good boys," adding, "We were all very close."

So he'd lied about being homeschooled. I didn't blame him, I guess. What was he supposed to say? "Hi, I'm eighteen and dead?"

I clicked on several other stories, most of them much the same.

One story, however, from a small independent Santa Fe newspaper, went into more depth than the others, and mentioned that the two young men had tragically lost their beloved father, a local rancher, in a random drive-by shooting in a grocery store parking lot when they were very young. A smiling photo of their handsome, kind-eyed father, Gregory Hartwell, jogged my memory.

The dream.

Gregory Hartwell was the man gunned down in the dream Travis had shown me. I remembered the children the man had pushed in the cart. Of course! The older one must have been Randy. He'd tried to save his father. The baby, that poor, dear, sweet little baby, must have been Travis.

I paused, with tears welling in my eyes, feeling incredibly stupid and guilty. I didn't know why it hadn't occurred to me before. It was so terribly sad. They'd been through so much. No wonder Randy was angry and an alcoholic! What child wouldn't be scarred for life having witnessed so terrible an act committed against his own father? He was, as my mother often called it, "self-medicating."

I looked at a few more stories. The photos of Travis and Randy revealed without a doubt that they were the young men I knew. It had to have been them. Their poor mother, I thought. She'd lost first her beloved husband, and then her only children. I wondered what she was doing now, how she had been able to go on.

I clicked on the earlier stories about Travis's rodeo competitions. It turned out that he had been the top tie-down roper in the state in his age group, and in the top three for that sport nationally, quite famous in those circles. He was also a talented fiddle player and singer, and often performed around the Southwest with his own alternative country band that, one of the pieces said, had been accepted to play at the prestigious South by Southwest festival in Austin, Texas, this year.

I wasn't surprised that Travis was that good at sports and music; he was clearly a skilled athlete, very coordinated, and he'd mentioned playing the fiddle. I was surprised he hadn't mentioned how good he was at any of these things, though. I'd bragged to him about being the top youth violinist in the city, and he'd acted impressed while never offering up his own accomplishments for me to marvel at.

I turned the computer off, feeling more unsettled than before. How could I be so proud of a guy who was dead? Why didn't he *feel* dead in my heart? I couldn't be hallucinating, like my mother said. And why was my pendant suddenly seeming to operate with a mind of its own?

I just didn't know anymore.

My stinging, squinty eyes began to shut. I turned off the lights, missing Buddy with a hollow sick feeling, fell sideways onto my bed, still wearing my boots, and drifted off into an instant, deep slumber.

It didn't last.

No sooner had I begun to dream of a beautiful boy at a rodeo on a perfect summer day, when I was awakened by the distinct sound of a determined fingernail, tap-tap-tapping on my bedroom window.

fourteen

I sat straight up in bed, my heart pounding, and listened. *Be careful.*

I heard the echo of Travis's whispered voice in my head, fading like the dream I'd just had. I couldn't remember the details, just a dream with Travis in it, and we were sitting near a pond.

Tap, tap, tap.

I took a labored, shallow breath.

Three taps, all in succession, played out in exactly the same rhythm each time. I sat paralyzed with fear. What could I do? Move? Not move? Scream? Run away? Crawl into bed with my mom? Nothing seemed right, other than sitting stock-still and hoping it'd go away.

Tap, tap, tap.

I'm here. It's okay.

Why could I hear Travis's voice now? Maybe I was still half asleep. . . .

Tap, tap, tap.

That was when I caught a faint glimmer of light in the corner of my room, near the beanbag. I looked, and saw a distinct shadow outline now, and it was in the shape of Travis.

"Travis!" I whispered, filled with mixed emotions. On the one hand, it was nice to know Travis was here with me. On the other hand, I was happy that I hadn't changed into my pajamas earlier, realizing I would have had an audience.

"Travis, what's happening?" I whispered.

The shadow morphed into the orb and zipped through the wall by the window, then came back in and faded into the ghost smoke, wrapping itself around me.

Tap, tap, tap.

Self-consciously, I got up and padded over to the window, lifting the edge of the curtain to peek outside.

There stood Logan, tall and strapping as ever in his yellow ski instructor parka, his handsome face illuminated a pale orange-yellow by the streetlamp down the road. His breath came in frigid, foggy clouds, and he hugged himself against the cold. In the high desert of New Mexico, the nighttime temperature could be as much as twenty or thirty degrees lower than the daytime temperature. I was sure he was freezing, and felt sorry for him. When he saw me peeking out, he smiled, and waved. I cracked the window.

"What are you doing here?" I asked, aware that I was being watched by Travis.

"You didn't answer my texts or return my calls," Logan said, stepping toward me, whispering. "I was really worried about you."

I realized I hadn't checked my phone since calling Kelsey on the drive back from Chaco Canyon.

I said to Logan, "Sorry. Dead battery." It was a lie, but innocent enough. "I'm fine. Just busy."

"Kelsey called me," he said with a concerned expression on his face. "She told me about your brain injury and hallucinations. I've been worried."

"She *what*?" I whispered furiously, anger filling my body.

"I've been trying to reach you. I wanted to make sure you were okay."

"I'm fine, no thanks to my supposed best friend."

"Can I come in?" he asked.

I balked. He'd never come here at night, or been in my room without my mom knowing it.

"Um, no. Sorry. I don't think that's a good idea," I said.

"Then can you come out for a minute?" he asked. "I

want to take a little walk and talk."

I glanced back at the digital clock on my nightstand. "Logan, it's three in the morning!"

"I know. I couldn't sleep, I was so worried about you. I . . . I think I love you, Shane."

It was the first time he'd ever said anything like this to me, and I did not know how to respond. I didn't love Logan. I liked him, but I did not love him. In fact, I knew in my heart that I was going to have to break up with him if I ever wanted to have anything with Travis. I didn't like hurting people's feelings, or accepting that I was in love with, you know, a *dead* guy, but it was inevitable that I'd have to do both, and soon.

"I appreciate that," I said, awkwardly, "but I'm really tired and I just want to go back to bed."

"I understand," he said, seemingly embarrassed that I hadn't returned his declaration of love. "Just a quick walk? Just up to the end of your street and back."

"My mom," I said worriedly. In truth, I was sure she'd be out cold. Whenever she drank wine, she was difficult to rouse.

"Please, Shane? I have a lot to tell you and I can't do it through a window in a whisper."

"Fine," I said, growing irritated, but also preferring the idea of talking to Logan away from Travis. I resolved to break things off with him right here, right now, because it needed to be done. It would be difficult, but easier done out there, in the cold, with a clear head.

Because I had fallen asleep in my clothes and boots, I simply shrugged into my jacket, removed the screen from the window as quietly as I could, and climbed out somewhat clumsily. I wondered if Travis would stay in the house, or come with me. I hoped he'd stay behind and give me some privacy. Travis and I had a lot to work out in this regard, I realized.

Logan helped me out of the window, then planted a big kiss on my lips. I felt awful, like I was cheating on Travis. I made a note of this, realizing that as crazy as it sounded, I felt more like Travis's girlfriend than Logan's. Our kiss, our touch was dull. I saw a wisp of smoke snaking through the wall and hovering just behind Logan. Travis was coming with me. He'd seen the kiss.

"Let's walk fast," I said, wanting to get this over with. "I'm freezing."

We moved stealthily across the yard, careful not to wake my mother or anyone else in the neighborhood, all the way to the driveway, and then down to the street. There was no one out, and the full moon was bright, lowering toward the west. Logan told me all about the conversation he'd had with Kelsey, and then came the shocker.

"I know everyone will probably tell you you're crazy," he said, trying to hold my hand, "but I want you to know that I've had some experiences lately that are kind of like what you're talking about."

"You have?" I asked, stunned. I pretended to be too cold to hold hands, and hugged myself. "Like what?"

"I can't really talk about them," he said, "because it sounds bad, I know it does, but I want you to know that I don't think you're crazy, with the souls and all that."

The determination I'd been hoping for to break up with Logan started to fade. He was the last person in the world I would have thought would believe me, especially after the way he had treated Travis at the bagel shop.

"Thanks, Logan," I said affectionately. But ultimately, this wasn't a good development, was it? This was making things harder.

We continued up the road, toward where it dead-ended at the foot of the mountain about two blocks away. The night was still and quiet and dark, but I saw the smoke and shadow of Travis curling and wafting through the frigid air alongside us. Logan, for all his talk of spirits, did not notice.

"What I can tell you is that I know what I know from hunting," Logan said. "I feel this incredible connection with something, or someone, bigger than me, every time I take an animal down."

I immediately disliked the sound in his voice. I could not relate to what he said because I'd never killed anything that I knew of, and had no desire to start. I remained quiet, and he began to talk animatedly, in a hypermasculine tone.

"It's just this animal instinct I can't explain," he said almost in a growl. Suddenly, I heard something crunch and rustle in the tumbleweeds just back from the road, near us. Logan noticed instantly, his eyes and body turning toward the noise, his hand reaching quickly into the pocket of his parka and extracting the obscenely large, weird knife he'd shown off earlier in the week. The weapon's blade glinted in the pale light of the streetlamp.

"What are you doing?" I asked, horrified.

"You hear that?" he asked, crouching wildly, with a crazy look in his eyes and a manic sound to his voice. "Something's out there. A rabbit, I bet. Perfect timing! This is what I mean. I'm so good at tracking, Shane. I don't want to brag, but I'm better at it than anyone I ever met. It's like what I was born for. I can smell the animals, feel their fear. I get a rush from it." I heard him take a deep breath as he stalked predatorily, and silently, toward the sound we'd heard, and I held my breath as he stood still, listening.

No more sound came.

"I didn't realize this was a hunting trip," I griped miserably, "or I would have stayed home." Any rekindled affection I might have felt for Logan a moment before was gone as quickly as it had come, replaced by disgust.

Logan returned to my side, apologizing. "It's just, when I hear an animal moving, instinct takes over my body. I can't explain it. The older I get, the stronger the instinct. It's a survival instinct, but it's God, too. I know it because I can feel the animal's spirit leave its body after the kill."

"Okay," I said doubtfully.

"Is that what it's like for you, seeing spirits?" He did not wait for me to answer, which was just as well. "Knowing that you hold the power of life or death over something, looking it in the eye, and feeling its energy, knowing there's more to life than what we can see with our eyes, and just knowing that you were sent here to partake of it, that you were meant to reap that energy for yourself—I feel powerful, you know? *Alive*. In control."

I looked at Logan and felt a heavy revulsion wash over me. I knew I liked burgers, but I did not understand this bloodlust Logan suddenly had.

"It's not like that for me," I said carefully. "But I think I hear what you're saying."

"It's just really liberating to be able to tell someone," Logan told me. "I knew there was a reason I was attracted to you, other than you being totally hot. Which you are." He paused and gave an attempt at a smoldering, sexy look, and then he whispered, "I want you so bad."

He pulled me toward him, and pressed me against his

body. I could feel his excitement, and it repulsed me. I pushed away from him, and he grabbed at me, grotesquely, aggressively. I had to jump out of the way to avoid his hands.

He grinned, thinking it was a game, and growled, "There are only two things that make me feel alive: sex and hunting. I never thought I'd be able to share them both with the same person, you know? We're soul mates, Shane. That's what this means."

I cringed at his use of the phrase *soul mates* because I knew it wasn't true. I also hated that he assumed I was going to go all the way with him. We'd never done it, and after hearing what he was saying tonight, I had lost any desire I might ever have had to do so with him. I also knew that it wasn't the time or place to say any of this to Logan, who seemed drunk on his own power in a way that chilled me to the bone.

Logan grabbed me and pulled me in to him, forcing a kiss onto my lips. I squirmed and tried to get out of his grip, but it was too strong. The harder I pulled back, the more ruthlessly he pressed my body against his. I felt his excitement again, rising against my leg, and was overcome with the urge to spit. I strained again to get away, but he wasn't having it. He forced me against him, and stuck his tongue into my mouth, and down my throat, so roughly I almost threw up. I twisted away from him, and he was about to grab me again when we heard the crunch of sticks underfoot, much louder now, just ahead of us, and then the sound of something sprinting off toward the empty expanse of land at the end of the cul-de-sac, toward the mountain.

"Oh, yeah," Logan said. "Wait here. I'm gonna show you what I mean. Here, bunny bunny bunny!"

With that, he darted off after whatever it was. I stood horrified at the side of the road, frozen with fear as he disappeared into the national forest land. I spit on the ground, and shook Logan's ugly energy off of me. I heard rustling, grunting, and other awful noises, snorting, and then a yelp of pain that wasn't human. What the heck was Logan doing? This was too strange, almost stranger than everything else I'd been through. I considered turning and running home, but something—I truly believed it was Travis, oddly enough—told me it would be better for me to stay right where I was.

Moments later, Logan returned, holding a large and very frightened-looking jackrabbit by the ears in one hand. In the other hand, he wielded the knife.

"Don't," I said. "Please, Logan. Stop this."

I watched in horror as Logan stuck the tip of the knife into the rabbit's belly, drawing blood and a panicked sort of shriek from the creature. I felt terrible, and wondered why Travis wasn't stopping this. Where was he? I looked for a sign of him, and couldn't find one.

"What is wrong with you?" I cried at Logan. "That poor animal hasn't done anything to you! Leave it alone!"

"It's there," he said, as though this were the obvious answer. "It's like the Bible says, man was put on earth to dominate all its creatures. Survival of the fittest."

"I don't think that's what the Bible says."

He shoved the knife in more, and the animal squirmed helplessly, suffering greatly.

"Stop!" I screamed, and charged Logan, knocking him to one side. He still clutched the knife in his hand, and the rabbit fell to the ground. Logan laughed.

"Man, that was awesome! I feel so alive. I saw his soul, Shane. You never see a soul as clearly as when something is afraid it's about to die. You see it then, in the eyes, getting ready to leave the body."

"I want to go home," I said, wholly creeped out now.

"Look," he said, showing me the coarse hairs and blood on his blade. "I took part of him with me."

"That's disgusting."

He ignored this. "I don't want to hunt with guns anymore. It's not enough anymore. I like to feel the flesh give way under my own hand. I know it sounds crazy, but it's a more intimate connection with the animal."

I turned and started walking toward my house, and said nothing. He chased after me.

"Hey, yo, I'm sorry," Logan said. "I didn't mean to offend you. I just thought, after what Kelsey told me about you seeing ghosts and dead people and all that macabre stuff, I figured you'd get it."

"Oh, I get it," I said, trembling.

"You do?" he asked, overjoyed.

"No. I mean, I get that we can't be together anymore," I said. I was terrified to make him angry, so I tried to let him down gently by lying to him. "I want to break up. I like you, you're a cool guy, but I don't think we're right for each other."

Logan was silent for a moment, and I heard him sheathe the knife. My shoulders dropped a little in relief.

Nervously, I looked around me for Travis. I caught a glimmer of lights in the area where the jackrabbit had fled and knew that Travis was saving the poor little animal, just as he'd saved me. My heart melted with love for him.

"Well, that was unexpected," Logan said with a hint of shame. "I thought you were cool with me the way I am."

"It's not you," I lied, trying to seem normal and maybe even a little dumb, instinct telling me it would be unwise to criticize Logan right now. "It's me. I'm going through a lot, and I appreciate your concern for me and all that, but right now I think I just need to be alone."

He looked angry. "I mean, damn, Shane. I don't know what to say. I just . . . I feel like a moron now."

I was silent.

He continued, "I just opened up for you like I never did for anyone. I said I loved you. I showed you my soul. My passion. And you rejected me. Ouch, man."

"I'm sorry. We can still be friends, okay?"

"You sure you want to break up?"

"Yeah."

"Weird. No girl ever broke up with me before. I'm actually a pretty popular guy. I mean, you might not dig me, but a lot of chicks do. I know that for a fact."

"I know," I said, actually pitying him for sounding so insecure now. "You're a great catch. You'll find someone new in no time."

"I'm not worried about that," he said, but he did, in fact, sound worried. "I bet I'll have a new chick by Kelsey's party. Just watch."

"Okay," I said, not caring one way or another if he ever found another "chick."

We walked the rest of the way to my house without speaking, and it was difficult for me to tell what, if anything, Logan was thinking. I thanked him for coming by, and told him I'd go the rest of the way from the street to the house by myself.

Logan puffed up his chest in a macho sort of way, and stalked off, down the road toward his own house, which was about a quarter mile from mine. Something told me to keep my eye on him, and so I stood and watched him retreat. It was dark, so I couldn't be sure my eyes weren't deceiving me, but when he got about a block away, I was almost certain I saw a dog or wolflike creature step out of the sagebrush between two houses and follow him. I thought to call out to him to warn him, but just as I was going to do so, the animal changed into a man, jogging to Logan's side, and touching his arm the way you did to get a stranger's attention. The man seemed to ask Logan a question, and Logan answered, then the two of them shook hands, and began to walk together, seeming to be talking animatedly.

Terrified anew, I turned back toward my house, and ran all the way to the window. I crawled back through it, replaced the screen, and, after reminding myself that Travis could get through the walls just fine if he wanted to, locked it all behind me. I settled back on the bed, shivering from cold and general weirdness. I stayed like that for a few minutes, and then, sure enough, the smoke seeped into the room again, condensed down to an orb, circled me a couple of times as though checking to make sure I was okay, and then went to hover, as smoke once more, near the beanbag.

"Did you help that poor bunny?" I asked.

I sat in silence for a moment, embarrassed. Nothing. No reply.

"I mean, I'm pretty sure you did. I saw you back there.

Thank you. Thank you for everything. When Logan said he loved me, I felt—I just felt like there was no way I could ever tell anyone those words, unless that someone was you. I hope that's okay."

The orb changed color now, from palest blue cycling through a rainbow of colors, before going back to blue, and then, seemingly exhausted by the effort, fading completely. Though I could no longer see him, I knew Travis was still there.

And I knew he loved me.

My belly twittered with butterflies and happiness. I squirmed a little, and giggled like a dork. I sat up in bed, searching for him in the darkness, but I saw nothing. I wondered if ghosts needed sleep, too.

Eventually, I flopped back down onto my pillow, and curled up on my side. That's when I sensed Travis lying next to me. I couldn't see his light, but I felt him, and knew he was there, behind me, on his side, too. I closed my eyes, and allowed myself to understand what I sensed. An arm slipping beneath my own, wrapping around my waist. His head on the pillow next to mine. The fronts of his legs and body spooned against the backs of mine. His breath, warm and comforting, on the back of my neck. His lips, brushing my nape. That electric pulse of happy energy through my soul from his.

And then, as I drifted toward sleep, his voice came to

me, true and strong in my mind, telling me I was safe, that everything was fine, that Buddy was still alive, that it was time for me to sleep now, that I'd worried too much, been through too much. That he was glad I knew about the rodeo and the music, that he was glad Logan was gone, that Victor was no longer near the house, that I was safe, safe, safe, that he was sorry for the difficulties he'd caused me, that he was so happy to have found me, that he'd never let me go, that his heart told him he loved me more than he'd ever loved anyone or anything in his existence, that he had never loved any girl like this, and that he knew I was his destiny, that whatever happened to me would happen to him, that he was mine forever if I wanted him.

It was pure, inexplicable madness, and at one level, I knew that. But at another, deeper, more profound level, a level without words, a level of music and vibrations alone, I also knew it was true, all of it, true as a melody.

I relaxed. For the first time in more than a week, I relaxed. I let go. I melted into the mattress, and felt suddenly, inexplicably at peace, and blissfully happy, utterly safe, as though nothing could ever go wrong from now on.

In that quiet, intoxicating, magical, romantic, half-asleep moment, curled up with my handsome ghost in the middle of the night, I let myself believe that because of Travis's love, only good things were coming for me from now on, that everything would work out for the best.

fifteen

I **dreamed of the rodeo.** It was a summer day, with a distant thunderstorm brewing on the western horizon. In New Mexico we called summer our monsoon season, and everyone just planned their days around the inevitable drenching, healing rains that afternoon or evening might bring.

I hovered again, disembodied but acutely aware of everything, this time above a small, rustic rodeo ring. People crowded onto the metal bleachers below me, eating hot dogs, drinking beers and sodas, fussing over babies, laughing with one another, and watching the activity in the ring with good cheer.

I floated a little higher, unseen by anyone here, and felt Travis with me again.

Farmington. It was his voice, telling me this. *New Mexico State Finals. June 21.*

My sixteenth birthday. I tried to remember what I'd done that day. I'd stayed at the emergency room with my mother, having just gotten back from a white-water rafting trip with Kelsey in the Rio Grande Gorge near Taos, a present from my mother. That day, she and the nurses had thrown a little surprise party for me at the nurses' station, with cake and presents.

At that moment, as the rodeo was under way.

I looked around me, and saw the bulls in their pens, and wondered if they knew the smell was of their own kind broiling. I saw young cowboys behind the chutes, joking with one another, eyeing one another with competitive glares.

Watch. This is where it starts. The rest of the story you need to know.

I saw Travis brushing a horse, dark like the one he rode when we first met, in an area that seemed to be the backstage of the arena. I watched him saddle it and put some kind of equipment on its legs, near the ankles. Next, he changed out of his jeans into another pair, these a bit roomier. He went to something that looked like a hatbox and took out some ropes, which he put baby powder on before gripping them to test their feel. He took some little ropes and put them over the saddle.

As Travis did this, some other men began loading five calves into chutes. Travis and some other young men took this as their cue to mount their horses and get into position. The announcer said the next event would be tie-down roping, and then I saw one of the calves dart into the ring. The calf was immediately chased by a young cowboy, not Travis. A matter of seconds later, the calf had been roped, and the cowboy had jumped off his horse and tied its legs together, ending by standing with his hands over his head. The crowd went nuts when the announcer said the cowboy had broken a record. The next four cowboys did the same thing, each near to or equaling the time of the first. Then, Travis was up. Astonishingly, he broke the record that had just been broken, moving with a breathtaking agility and confidence. The crowd went ballistic.

No one in the crowd went crazier than Randy, whom I spotted tucking his half-pint bottle back into his shirt in order to stick two fingers into his mouth for the occasional shrill whistle of elation.

"That's my little brother!" I heard him shouting, punching the air as all the other young cowboys began to slap Travis on the back in congratulations. "I knew it. I knew it."

Travis took his horse, led him to a trailer in the back lot, and gave him an apple, patting his nose.

I watched as Travis then walked through the crowd,

a breathtakingly beautiful smile on his handsome face, accepting their accolades with a humble, but triumphant, grin. I watched as he went to find Randy, taking the bleacher stairs three at a time. He went directly to his brother for a manly hug and some more back slapping.

The brothers stood, arm in arm, waving to friends and celebrating the victory, and then, suddenly, Randy's face fell into a numb, confused expression. Travis noticed, and asked him what was wrong. Randy didn't answer, and seemed paralyzed for a moment, in shock.

I watched as Travis, concerned, followed the line of his brother's gaze to the sinister face of a man across the ring from them, who sat alone in the bleachers on the other side. He wore a dirty black cowboy hat and had light eyes and a distinctive black mustache. He had a strong but narrow jaw with a dent hacked into the middle, a slash of a scar on his left cheek, and rather large ears for his size. He was middle-aged, maybe in his early fifties, but sinewy and strong, and wearing a blue denim shirt that showed off his broad shoulders.

The longer Randy looked at the man, the darker, redder, and angrier his face became. The man drank carelessly from a bottle of beer, and his small, green, beady eyes kept turning back to the brothers with a look of eerie humor in them, before quickly darting away again in smug satisfaction. The man stood, and made a big show out of stretching, yawning, and scratching his private parts, almost as if to prove to the watching boys that he didn't care about them, or anybody there, or simple manners, and he wasn't in any rush. He was taking his time moseying along on his own terms.

Down I drifted in my disembodied state, closer to Travis and Randy, close enough to touch them now, though they could not see me at all, of course.

"That's him," Randy said, his voice quaking with emotion as he bounced angrily on the balls of his feet, the way guys in movies did when they were hoping for a fight.

"Who?" Travis asked, confused.

"Him—that's the dude who shot Daddy."

"What?" Travis said, stunned, squinting toward the man again. "How do you know?"

"He looks the same. Exactly the same. Look at him! How could you forget a jacked-up face like that?"

"I was freakin' one year old."

"I was six. I remember it. That's the guy."

"Are you sure?" Travis asked, worry creasing his brow. "It's been seventeen years, man."

But Randy didn't answer, because the man with the mustache was on the move, walking casually toward the dirt parking lot, weaving his way through the crowd. Randy gave chase, weaving through the throng on this side of the ring, hopping up now and then to make sure he still had the man in his sight, motoring forward with fierce determination in his eyes.

"Randy!" Travis called. "Wait up!"

Randy barreled on, ignoring his brother. Travis cursed under his breath, and began to follow him, moving with a fast agility that impressed me, and stirred in me an urge to touch him.

My heart was thundering. Something bad was coming, I could sense it. I floated, following Travis as he hurried to Randy's side. Randy wriggled through the bodies in between them now, practically climbing over people in his haste.

"Slow down. Calm down, Randy!" Travis said, trailing just a foot or two behind him. People in the crowd watched them with concern, wondering what could have taken the day's champion from the heights of glory to the depths of the despair apparent on his face now.

"That's the guy," Randy repeated, his fury bearing traces of a sadistic sort of joy. "I been waiting a long time for this day. Oh, yeah. This is so on."

The man with the mustache noticed the brothers following him, and his deliberately nonchalant expression changed, upon reaching the dirt lot, to one of evil pleasure. He was baiting them. He wanted to be followed. With a quick look over his shoulder, he began to trot across the lot, toward an old black Chevy pickup truck. I gasped when I recognized the truck. I knew instantly that Randy was right. This was the man who'd shot their father.

Together, the brothers trailed him, matching the pace, and before the man could jump into the Chevy, they got into a large four-door silver Ford pickup truck, with the trailer hooked to the back, containing Travis's horse. Randy took the driver's seat. Down I floated, until I was hovering in the backseat of the truck itself, watching as Travis begged Randy to calm down and think this through. Randy wasn't hearing it. He was on a mission, in a daze. He gunned the engine, a crazed look on his face, and with the truck lurching in his anger, followed the black Chevy as it peeled out of the lot and down the frontage road, to the west, toward the entrance to the Interstate.

"Slow down, dammit," Travis begged his brother. "Scooter's in the back. You'll injure him."

"Just shut up," Randy said, anger in control of him now. "For once in your life, just stop talking."

"You don't even know if that's the guy!"

"Just shut up!" Randy repeated, shouting. "I know that's him."

"Why would he come here?" Travis asked. He looked back at the trailer in worry. "You're going to hurt my horse, dammit."

"Did you see the way he was looking at us?" Randy asked. "He wanted us to see him! He was taunting us. He came for us."

"You sound crazy."

"Plenty of things sound crazy. It sounds crazy to be a little kid and see your daddy shot in the middle of the parking lot right in front of you, too. Right? *Right?*"

Travis didn't answer.

"Yeah, that's crazy, right? But you know what?" Randy's eyes brimmed with tears now. "It happened. It happened. And you know what else? Huh? Now it's gonna unhappen." Randy smiled crazily. "It's time to make things right. Set things right for Daddy."

"That won't fix anything," Travis said. "You can't bring him back. Slow down before you ruin Scooter."

The Ford was on the freeway now, sprinting powerfully after the black Chevy as it sped to the north, in and out of lanes with reckless abandon. Travis held on to the bar near the window, clearly afraid for his safety, but Randy's eyes were glazed over with bloodthirsty vengeance and pain.

"Shut up, Travis! You don't remember it like I do. You were too little. You don't have that day burned into your brain like I do. You don't have nightmares like I do." Randy was screaming now, like a madman in the middle of a breakdown.

"You're going to kill us driving like this. Please. Pull over."

"I told you to shut up!" screamed Randy, driving faster.

"Just get his license plate number and report it to the

police. You're better than this, Randy."

"Seriously, Travis, if you don't shut up, I'm tempted to push you the hell out of this truck. You understand me?"

Travis stared at his brother in shock and, seeing that he was serious, realized there was no point in trying to reason with him.

"How much did you drink?" Travis asked him.

"A little."

"At least let me drive, Randy. You're gonna crash."

"What? And lose him again? Hell no, man. He won't get away with it. I'm on his tail, and I'm gonna stay there until this idiot pulls the hell over, or runs out of gas."

"Yeah?" Travis asked, starting to panic. "And then what're you gonna do? Huh? You want a repeat of what happened to Daddy? If this is really the guy, like you say it is, you want him to shoot us, too?"

"Then I'm gonna get even, that's what," Randy answered, sounding like a wounded child. "You think I ain't packin' too?"

"This is stupid," Travis said, exasperated and desperate. He produced a pen and a pad of paper from the glove box, and wrote down the license plate number on the Chevy. "Turn around. Just let the police handle it."

"Right, like they handled it the first time? They didn't do anything, Travis. He's still out there. He's right there. The man who killed our daddy is right in front of us! And it's partially your fault. We had to get you diapers, right? You had to crap your goddamned pants."

Travis stared at the black Chevy, tears welling in his eyes. "I was one year old, Randy."

"I don't care! You ruined everything. Do you know how many times I've wondered what it might have been like if you'd never been born? If you were never born, Daddy'd still be here."

Travis turned away from Randy, looking out the window at the desolate desert landscape speeding past. He didn't speak, fighting tears. Minutes passed, and still the Ford bore down upon the Chevy.

My heart was heavy, knowing how this would end, but not knowing exactly how it would get there. I watched, riveted, sickened, and tremendously sad for both of them. I wanted to reach down and pluck Travis out of that situation, but I was utterly helpless. On they drove, along the desolate road I'd come to know so well, chasing, driving right into the heart of a huge, deep, dark thunderstorm, into the pelting rain and deafening thunder, through the slashes of lightning, on and on, until mile marker 111, and then the turnoff for the dirt road to Chaco Canyon.

The newer Ford was much better equipped for the bumpy dirt road than the old black Chevy, which crawled over the holes in the mud, scraping its belly like a sick dog. Randy drove close to the car, so close at times that he rammed into it. Finally, the Chevy turned off the dirt road, into a steep, narrow dirt driveway that led down a hill, around a curve, and past several hills. It was utterly isolated here. No one around.

"So this is where the snake's been hiding out," mused Travis dejectedly, realizing that he was powerless to talk sense into his drunk, angry, emotionally distraught brother.

The Chevy stopped next to a filthy, decrepit single-wide mobile home. It was white, but stained and dented at odd angles, the roof and base painted red. The effect was like one big Cheshire cat smoker's smile nestled in the dirt. Beer bottles littered the yard, and the windows of the trailer were hung with ripped, stained children's sheets with cartoon characters on them.

"Nice little place he has here," Travis said sourly.

That was when the man got out of the Chevy and dashed through the punishing rain, into the trailer. I saw the black gun in his hand, and my heart began to race anew. I felt sick. I wanted to scream at the boys to turn around before it was too late, to go home. But I was helpless. It had already happened. There was nothing I could do now to change it.

Randy cut the Ford's engine, and reached under the driver's seat, pulling out a gun.

"Don't," Travis said.

Randy ignored him with a lunatic smile splashed across his face.

He opened the door, and dropped out of the truck. Travis sat in the cab for a moment, weighing his options.

"This isn't happening," he said to himself, making the sign of the cross on his chest. "God help us."

Travis began to recite the rosary, and stepped out of the car, jogging over to where Randy stomped through the rain, and standing behind him. I floated alongside him, watching as Randy strode powerfully, methodically to the thin metallic front door, and kicked it in.

Randy stepped in, holding the gun in front of him. It was now that I noticed him trembling a little. Randy, for all his bravado and anger, was afraid.

In I floated, alongside Travis. The living room was filthy, piled high with trash and dirty clothes. It smelled rancid. Drug paraphernalia and pornography littered the floor. The walls were the only neat thing about the place, and this only because they were plastered end to end with news stories about the murder of Gregory Hartwell. This man celebrated their father's death.

"Believe me now?" Randy asked his brother, as they took it all in.

"Jesus," Travis answered, horrified by the scene. "What is this place?"

The man with the mustache sat calmly on a trashy

plaid sofa, minus his shirt, polishing his gun as though he didn't have a care in the world. When he looked up at the brothers, he had a filthy smile on his face, his green eyes twinkling with sadistic delight. It was now that I saw how clearly his eyes resembled Randy's.

"So glad you came," he said, and I recognized the voice instantly. It was the same voice that had growled and panted at me on my cell phone in the Vortex, the same voice that had threatened to "git" me. I was struck numb with horror.

"Before I blow your freakin' head off, you wormy coyote, tell me your name," Randy demanded, pointing his gun at the man's head.

The man seemed unconcerned, and did not point his own gun back. He kept polishing it. "You don't have the cojones, Randy," he said, as though they were old acquaintances.

"How do you know my name, loser?" Randy roared.

"News stories," said the man, jutting his dimpled chin toward the stories taped to the walls. "I've been watching you." The man looked Randy up and down. "Keeping tabs on my experiment."

"What experiment?" Randy asked.

"Don't fall for it," Travis told him. "He's manipulating you. Don't talk to him anymore."

"You know what's struck me the most?" the man oozed

in a sleazy tone, smirking at Randy and winking at him in an almost seductive, sickening way. "I could never get over how different you two boys were. How you gave up, Randy, and lost yourself in whiskey and dope. Probably blamed yourself for me shooting your ole man. Like you should have saved him, right? You were the big boy, after all."

Randy's face fell in devastated recognition.

The man kept talking. "*Travis,* though. You're a chip off the old block."

Randy's shaking escalated. "Don't you talk about my daddy," he cried. "Don't! You're not fit to speak my father's name. You're nothing. You're lice. You're scum. Or you were scum; you're dead meat now."

Randy cocked the gun, and the man just smiled placidly.

"Oh, I'll talk about Travis's ole man. He was the worm who took your mother away from me. Your mother, boys, now there's a beautiful woman." He made a big show out of licking his lips. "She shoulda picked me, you know. She didn't. I've been watching her ever since, figuring ways to break her, and she never broke. That's why I killed him, if you wanted to know. To break that damn woman he took from me. It didn't work. She's rawhide tough, your mama, but juicy, delicious."

Randy and Travis exchanged a look of sudden

confusion, and then hideous understanding that this man had somehow been involved with their mother. That was when Travis snarled two words to his brother, very clearly and calmly: "Kill 'im."

"He can't," the man said smoothly to Travis. He turned his eyes to Randy. "Not if your daddy was a Hartwell." He paused and smiled. "But if you were *my* boy? Ah. A different story."

With that, Randy, gnashing his teeth, his eyes open wide in fury, pulled the trigger. The bullet entered the man's shoulder, a bit off the mark. Surprised, but in a delighted sort of way, the man looked at his wound and seemed to feel no pain.

"Well, well," he said with a calm chuckle. "Would you look at that. Maybe you're not a complete embarrassment to your father. But you can't aim for crap, drunk as y' are, you goddamned wuss."

"Screw you!" Randy screamed, firing off another round.

The bullet entered the man's belly this time, and again the man smiled, still unworried, and newly impressed, touching the gushing blood with his hands as if it were nothing but water from a lazy faucet.

"You have terrible aim, Randy," he said. "But I do commend you on your ambition. And for the record, because you asked, and because you've earned it now, my name is Victor. Victor Velarde. But my friends call me Green Eyes.

You look like me. I'm proud of you, Randy. Son. It will break your beautiful mama's heart to know you did this. I broke you, and now you will break her for me."

Randy said nothing. He just fired the gun, calm and steady, this time sending the bullet right between Victor's eyes, perfectly in synch with an enormous flash of lightning and simultaneous clap of thunder that came from quite nearby. The body slumped to the side, eyes still open, a nasty, sickening smile still writhing upon its lips. Victor Velarde was dead.

In a trance of sorts, Randy walked over to the man, gun still held out, and began to pump another round into his lifeless body.

"That's for Daddy," he said, sobbing.

"No," Travis said, touching Randy's arm gently. "That's enough. It's done."

"I hate him. I hate what he did. I hate what he said. It's not true. I'm *not* his son. It can't be."

"I know," Travis said. "It's not true. Guys like that just talk."

"May he rot in hell."

"We gotta get out of here." Travis pulled Randy's arm urgently, as the thunder boomed and lightning sliced the darkening sky.

"Why, Travis?" Randy sobbed, falling to his knees now, all his strength drained out of him. "Why'd he do it?"

Travis hoisted his brother up from the floor, dragged the slack and spiritless weight of Randy to a wearied standing position. "You're my brother. It doesn't matter what that animal said. Let's go. *Now.*"

The boys hurried away from Victor's body, and I was left to watch something that they did not see. A dark, putrid smoke came from the corpse of Victor, and snaked across the sofa, toward the wall, and into the outlet.

sixteen

I awoke at dawn, a scream strangling in the back of my throat. For a moment, I was so disoriented I couldn't remember where I was. I sat up in bed, my mouth dry as cotton, and looked around me with my heart doing double time. My bedroom. I was in my bedroom.

I took a deep breath and rubbed my eyes, which were nearly as dry as my mouth, trying to relax and clear my head from the nightmare. I couldn't get the gruesome image of Victor's rubbery, bloodied corpse slumped over on that ugly plaid sofa out of my head. He had deserved to die, but I didn't need to see it happen. It was too much.

When I looked at the pink beanbag, I saw the pale outline of Travis, near Buddy's empty dog bed. He glowed a little, his image coming in waves, vibrations, like the fading and reappearing rings on a pond after a stone is tossed in, almost as though he was fussing until he got comfortable.

The sun was just starting to paint the sky beyond the mountains a shade of palest yellow, and I guessed that the stronger the day became, the more solid Travis's outline would grow. Fifteen minutes later, the shape material-ized, and Travis's body appeared, lounging in my room, his hands behind his head, his feet planted on the white Berber carpet, knees bent and semi-far apart. He was hot, whole, and human again, staring back at me with a mel-ancholy smile that indicated he had no idea how alluring his physical position was to me. Though a little bit sleepy-looking and rumpled, he was as gorgeous as I remembered, and I waved, like a dork, not knowing quite what else to do—or at least smart enough to stop myself from doing all the things I wanted to do to him, in my mind.

"Mornin'," he whispered. He looked sad and worried.

"Good morning. What's wrong?" I asked.

"I've been thinking," he said.

I waited for him to say more. After a long moment, he did.

"It's not fair to you," he said.

"What's not?"

"This," he said, pointing to himself and then to me. "Us, all of this."

I tried to think of an answer, but I wasn't sure what he was saying, and told him so.

"I'm saying that after I get your dog back—and I will—the best thing for us would be if I just left you alone. I shouldn't be this far from my spot anyway."

"Your haunting spot?"

He nodded.

"You can't just leave me now," I told him as tears pooled in my eyes.

"After I find the dog," he said. "I owe you that, at least."

"Why are you talking like this?" I asked. "I felt you next to me here last night! I know you care about me. Don't try to deny it!"

Travis sighed heavily, pushed himself to his feet, and walked over to join me on the bed, sitting stiffly on the side, seeming to feel as awkward about the situation as I did.

"It's because I care about you that I have to leave you," he said. It looked for a moment as if he might be fighting back his own tears.

"That doesn't make any sense!" I protested.

He looked defeated and fatigued. "Look, think about it. Since meeting me, you've had nothing but problems, Shane."

"That's not true!"

"Your mom thinks you're crazy," he listed, counting on his fingers, "and your best friend is afraid you've gone off the deep end. You lost your boyfriend, and Victor took your dog. I think Victor's in touch with Logan now, too, which makes that guy even more dangerous to you. It's not good, Shane. All because of me."

"The man in the street . . . ," I said, my eyes filling with fear.

"Demons like Victor look for weak souls to use in this world. He's watching everything you do. Trying to find a way to get to me. It can only get worse, unless I disconnect from you."

I shook my head, and a tear fell.

He looked at me with a deep and agonized apology in his eyes.

"I can't do this to you," he said. "It was stupid of me. I shouldn't have come for you."

"No!" I said in an intense whisper, worried that if I yelled at him like I wanted to, I might wake my mother. "You should have! You should have come for me! We belong together, and you know it."

He nodded. "But maybe not right now. Maybe in another place and time. Maybe we were already together in some other dimension. I don't know. But what I do know is that you've lost too much because of me, and I can't stand it. I want you to be happy, Shane. And safe."

"I am happy with you," I told him. "And I don't care about losing Logan. We were bound to break up anyway."

"But Kelsey," he said.

"She'll come around. She always does." I wasn't sure I believed this, though.

"Buddy," he suggested.

"You said you'd get him back."

Travis sighed, and looked down at his hands. We stayed quiet for a while, thinking, and then I remembered the dream from last night and tried to change the subject, hoping he wouldn't bring it up again or follow through on abandoning me.

"Randy killed Victor," I said.

Travis turned his eyes to me, the sadness still in them, and nodded. "I thought I owed you an explanation of all this," he said. "I had to show you. I didn't want you thinking we were terrible people."

"That's the bad thing you did," I said, and felt tears stinging behind my eyes. "Being there when he did it?"

Travis nodded. "I told him to do it," he said. "I knew it was wrong, but I was so angry and filled with hate. I didn't stop him. That's how I ended up in the Vortex.

"Victor hasn't stopped trying to destroy us just because we've all died. If anything, he's worse now. He's doing everything he can to make sure we don't get to the Afterworld, because if we do, then there's a chance our mama will see us again someday. That's his mission, to punish her through us, to ruin her for all eternity."

"I'm sorry," I told him, feeling sick and sorrowful, resisting the overwhelming urge to embrace him and cover his face with kisses. "I'm sorry you had to go through all that."

Travis's eyes met mine, and he blinked, slowly, seeming to work hard to keep his composure. "I want you to know that Randy's not a bad guy," he insisted. "I know some people, all they see is the drinking and the drugs, they might think he's bad, but he's not. Deep down, he's a good guy. He used to be a happy kid, before all that. He blames himself. I know he does. He thinks he could have stopped it."

"He's got a lot of pain," I offered. "I can understand it, I guess. But still, he killed a man."

Travis's expression grew bitter. "If you can call Victor a man, sure he did. Victor has no conscience. He's pure evil. My brother killed a monster."

"It was premeditated murder, Travis."

"I realize that. But he was drunk, and he wasn't thinking straight."

"Why did you tell him to do it?" I asked.

Travis shook his head and buried his face in his hands, an uncharacteristically desperate and childish gesture for him. He looked up, tortured. "I wish I didn't. Not a day goes by that I don't regret it. But when he started talking as if he should have been our father—or was Randy's—I couldn't take it."

"I don't blame you," I said. "I would have probably

done the same thing."

"It's hard for me to talk about. It was easier to show you," he said, looking down at his hands again.

"You think Victor has Buddy?"

Travis nodded. "Of course."

"Do you think Buddy's alive?"

Travis nodded. "Buddy's bait. Victor wants to make me screw up somehow. He wants to tempt me into messing up so badly I end up where he is."

I felt incredibly torn now, as though I had to choose between saving my beloved dog and saving Travis from Victor. Travis seemed to sense this.

"I'm going to get your dog back, no matter what you say," he told me. "It's my fault Buddy ended up there."

"Where?" I asked.

"I think he's probably got him out at the trailer where Randy shot Victor. He haunts it. I'm going to start by checking there."

"That will be dangerous," I said.

Travis tried to shrug it off. "I'll take Randy with me, and a couple other guys we know from the Vortex. We're a lot smarter than Victor. Don't worry."

I began to cry, and he held me. His touch felt insanely good.

"What happened after you guys left the trailer that day?" I asked.

"We died."

"I know. But how? What happened, exactly?"

"I didn't show you our own deaths, Shane," he said, "because I didn't want you to see that."

"Oh."

"But I can tell you. A few minutes after Randy killed Victor, we were trying to get out of there. I was driving. We came around a bend in the dirt road, and there was Victor, plain as day, without a scratch, just standing in the middle of the road. I swerved on instinct and lost control. The truck and horse trailer—we all sailed off the road, over a little cliff there. We had propane in the back, and when we hit, the whole thing blew, like a nuclear bomb."

"Your horse died too?"

"Yeah."

"Is he what you were riding when you found me?"

"Yes."

My eyes welled with tears, and I couldn't help but let out a sob.

Travis put his free hand on top of our joined hands, and the heat and light came, entering through my skin and bones, filling me with a sense of calm—and temptation.

"Man, that feels good," he breathed.

"Too good," I said, shivering with pleasure.

We sat in silence for a moment, just enjoying each

other's energy, and the ways our bodies reacted to it. I didn't know what sex felt like yet, but if it was anything like holding hands with Travis, I was looking forward to the day I might find out.

"It's okay, you know," Travis told me. "Us killing Victor. If it hadn't happened this way, I might never have met you, we might never have shared this." He looked at our hands wistfully. "One thing I've learned is that everything really does happen for a reason. Even the things that seem bad turn out good, and the other way around, too."

"So maybe all this bad stuff you say is happening to me is really good stuff, then," I said.

"Maybe," he admitted. "But . . ."

I watched his mouth as he spoke. Again, I was taken by its perfection. He noticed me looking, and pulled back from me, almost imperceptibly, but kept his eyes on my face.

"You're real pretty," he said, seeming to weaken on his position to avoid me for my own good. "Even first thing in the morning."

I blushed, and realized my breath was probably as out of control as the mascara that was undoubtedly making raccoon circles under my eyes.

"Did it hurt a lot when you died?" I asked him.

Travis shook his head. "Didn't feel a thing, actually," he said. "It was more like—"

Down the hall, we heard sounds of hungover life in the kitchen as my mother rummaged around clumsily, slamming cabinet doors it sounded like, and dropping pots on the floor.

"You can't be here," I interrupted him, realizing in a panic that my mom would flip out if she saw him. Then again, she might believe me if she saw him, I thought. No, actually, she wouldn't. She would assume he was some stalker guy I was letting in through my window.

"You have to go," I said.

"Okay." His eyes went to the window I'd crawled out of last night to be with Logan. "Meet me outside in a little while."

"Where?"

"Same place Logan hurt the rabbit last night, end of the street."

There was a knock on my bedroom door then, and my mother's voice calling out, "Shane? Are you talking to someone in there?"

"I'm on speakerphone, Mom!" I cried, the lie coming quickly and easily now that I was starting to get the hang of it. "Talking to Logan."

My doorknob rattled as she tried to open the locked door.

"You know I don't like when you lock me out," she said.

"I know, hang on, I'll be right there. Let me—um, just let me end this call. Privacy, please."

Travis went soundlessly to the desk, and wrote on a piece of paper, "Come as soon as you can." His handwriting was small, tight, neat.

I nodded at him.

"You want pancakes?" my mother asked through the door. "And chicken-apple sausage? I have to get to work today—Dr. Paulson just called in sick—but I wanted to at least have breakfast with you before I go."

"Um, sure, Mom. That sounds great!" I answered far too enthusiastically, happy that she was leaving so that I could meet Travis without having to think up a lie for her. I hoped she wouldn't notice the happy tone, or that if she did, that she would just attribute it to my having ostensibly hit my head in the crash. Come to think of it, the whole "Shane hit her head" thing was going to come in handy for excusing all sorts of behaviors I might have gotten in trouble for in the past. Silver linings.

Travis smiled at me, winked to let me know everything was going to be okay. Then he walked through the wall of my room as though it weren't there, and was gone.

seventeen

After my mother had fed me some truly delicious pancakes with real maple syrup and butter, fussed over me in her usual guilt-ridden way, and assured me that she was going to set up another appointment at the hospital for my "brain issues," she left for work with the unwelcome announcement that my grandmother would be coming down from Truchas to watch me for the rest of the day. I felt sick.

"It's not that I don't trust you, sweetie," my mother said as she delivered a kiss to the top of my head. "We just need to be careful right now."

Nice.

I was desperate to see—and *feel*—Travis again, and to convince him not to disappear. I was already craving him and frantic at the thought of losing the guy who felt, in every way I could imagine, like my perfect other half. My soul mate. My Kindred.

Happily, however, I took a moment and did the math. Truchas was a good two-hour drive from Albuquerque, and my mother had only gotten called into work an hour ago, giving me a one-hour window in which to see whatever it was that Travis wanted to show me, and return to the house to play crazy invalid Shane for my granny.

As soon as I heard the garage door whirring shut behind my mother's Lexus, I hurried to clean up and get dressed, and went outside, running to the end of the street with the terrible fear I might never see Travis again.

Thankfully, I saw Travis standing about sixty feet into the national forest, already on the hiking trail that wound all through the foothills leading up to Sandia Peak. I hurried to meet him.

"You made it." Travis hugged me as though we hadn't seen each other in years, rather than just one short hour ago.

"You can't leave me," I said. "I won't let you. I'm not some fragile little girl. Whatever this is, whatever we are, I can handle it. I promise you."

"Let's walk," he said. "I have something to show you."

I followed him along the trail. A few others were out on the trails, the die-hard runner types mostly, in their protective winter gear. They didn't give Travis a second glance, assuming him to just be a regular human.

We walked for maybe ten minutes, when Travis suddenly stopped and knelt down to look beneath some dried sagebrush. I watched as he extracted a small animal from under the plant. It was a baby cottontail rabbit, bleeding and terrified, broken and handicapped, half frozen to death. I felt sick and sorry for it, and turned away. I had seen enough misery and gore lately. I couldn't take any more.

"Hey, little guy," Travis said calmly, his voice warmly reassuring. "Let's take a look at you. What happened here? A coyote tried to get you, huh? Big, mean coyote. We won't let him get away with it, will we?"

The rabbit made a tiny, frightened screeching sound.

"Can I look yet?" I called out, knowing what he was up to.

"Still a little gross," Travis answered. "But not for long, eh, little fella?"

A minute or so later, Travis instructed me to turn around. There, in his lap, was a whole, happy, healthy baby bunny. He released the animal, and off it sprinted, in a zigzagging line given to it by nature for the best shot at avoiding the mouths of predators, lightning fast.

"So basically, you go around rescuing roadkill?" I joked. He appreciated my sick humor and cracked a grin.

"And the occasional pretty girl."

"You have more than one?" I asked flirtatiously.

"Nope. One's plenty." He seemed almost insulted by the question. "I'm pretty sure there's only one like *you*, anyway."

We walked on, mostly in silence now as the hike got steeper and my breath got heavier. Finally, we came to a stone bench in the middle of the path. We were the only ones around. The bench faced out over a beautiful little canyon.

"Look at this view. I love it here." He took a deep breath.

"This is very pretty," I said as the damp cold of the bench seeped into my legs and seat. I paused. "Tell me you're not going to leave me."

"I brought you here for a reason," he told me, standing up again. "Because I don't want your last memory of me to be a sad one. I want us to do something fun together before we part ways."

I began to cry with frustration and desperation. "We're not parting ways! Quit saying that."

He seemed to feel sorry for me, but he was resigned. "Let's have a little fun. Good memories."

I looked at him quizzically.

"Remember how I told you I have different ways of traveling? Well, I wanted to show you how I get around

189

when I'm in a hurry or have a long way to go," he said. "I can bring living humans with me, if I want."

I shook my head and blinked, a little confused because we were standing perfectly still.

Travis explained. "I use memorials. It can be a gravestone, or a *descanso* by the side of the road, or something like this. Anything that someone has built in loving memory for someone who has moved on to the next plane, I can use it. All revenants can."

"Use it how?"

"I'm about to show you. C'mere."

Gingerly, I stood beside him as he wrapped his arms around me. Travis grinned in his gorgeous way, and told me to hold on to him. I obliged, and was sorely tempted by the nearness of him. I wanted to nuzzle into his neck, to kiss it, but instead I just embraced him. He seemed to focus on something in the distance, and looked almost as though he was entering a trancelike state. I felt a deep, dark vibration in my solar plexus, and the world seemed to shift somehow, just a little, like when you are suddenly dizzy for a brief second.

"Here we go," he said, as the wind kicked up around us, enveloping us in a small, warm tornado that was filled with golden waves of light. I felt the bench drop out from below my feet, and we hovered for a moment, with Travis holding me tightly to him with both arms now. And then we spun, and soared. I squealed a little, and pressed the side of my face into his chest. I tried to look down, but I couldn't see anything at all anymore, other than the golden light and white fog of the tornado. I squeezed my eyes shut for a moment, gathered my courage, and opened them again to find Travis smiling at me. My belly felt the way it did on a roller coaster when it dropped. It was completely thrilling and exciting, and I laughed out loud.

"Get ready to land," Travis said. Again, I closed my eyes, anticipating a bump. But no bump came.

When I opened my eyes, the tornado has dissipated. I was still in Travis's arms, but we weren't in the foothills near my house anymore. Only a few seconds had passed, but we were somehow now on the side of Highway 550, at mile marker 111, in the bright blazing light of the winter morning, next to Travis's and Randy's *descansos*. My feet were on the ground. It was real. I twisted out of Travis's grasp, and spun, looking about me in shock. I knelt and touched the ground, ran my finger over the white wood of the cross, amazed to be here.

Travis chuckled, apparently delighted by my discombobulation, and by the fact that he had someone special to share his world with now.

"Isn't that cool?" he asked.

"How does it work?" I demanded. "Why don't people know about this?"

Travis cocked his head to get a better look at me with those unflinchingly beautiful eyes, finding great humor in my astonishment. "Most people don't hang out with revenants, or if they do, the revenants are usually better at keeping secrets from them. But I like sharing my secrets with you."

"Then you can't abandon me."

"We'll see," he said as he grinned. He was so beautiful, so happy, so alive. I stood still, just looking at the way the sun found golden flecks in the brown of his eyes. I wanted him with a profound ache. He came closer, and brushed the back of his hand lightly against my cheek.

"It is tempting," he told me softly, "so tempting to kiss you."

"I wish you would."

His face registered pain, and he sighed heavily. "No."

He ran his fingertips beneath my chin, very lightly, and down my neck, to my collarbone. I shivered with pleasure, and closed my eyes.

"But I love you," I whispered.

"I love you, too," he said.

Then he pulled away from me, and began to tickle me, switching gears. I opened my eyes to see him laughing at me playfully, with a naughty sort of smile.

"You *suck*!" I tickled back.

He laughed, and dodged my hands. I lunged again,

and dug my fingers into his sides. He doubled over, clearly quite ticklish.

"Aha! So you do have a weakness!" I said.

"Stop!"

I kept tickling him, enjoying having some small power over his body. "Beg me," I said.

"Please, please, *please* stop tickling me!" he called out, laughing so hard tears streamed from the corners of his eyes.

"Fine," I said, backing off. We both panted from the exertion, and regarded each other with longing and happiness.

"That sucked," he said, still laughing a little. "I hate being tickled."

Something occurred to me now. "If you can be tickled, is your body just like a regular body when you're a revenant?"

"What do you mean?" he asked.

"I mean, you must be hungry. I should have offered you breakfast."

"I'm okay. I'll get something in a bit."

"Can you feel pain, too? Can you bleed and break bones and die . . . again?"

"Sort of." He grimaced and seemed surprised I'd asked this. "Yeah. This body can, I mean. Why? You want to hurt me now?" He grinned to show he was kidding.

"No! I was just wondering, like, because of Victor and all that, what if you got killed again?"

"Then I'd forfeit my right to redemption."

I didn't understand.

"I'd go immediately to the Underworld," he elaborated. "Poof, gone. So I have to be careful. Good thing you can't die from tickling."

My eyes were wide. I looked around and said, "Are you safe here?"

"Don't worry about me. This is supposed to be fun, remember? Come here."

I went to him, and he held me again, harder than before, and asked me to think of a place somewhere in New Mexico.

"Carlsbad Caverns," I said.

He got that distant look in his eyes again, and again I felt the low humming in my chest.

"Coming right up," he said. "Hang on tight."

I kept my eyes open. The world around us began to move, the way it does when you're on a carousel, faster and faster, and as the gold-and-white tornado appeared around us, I giggled, and tried to push away from him, to touch the undulating lights, but he grabbed me, hard, with a stern look.

"Do not let go of me, whatever you do," he said. "Not here."

I heeded the advice, and clung to him. In short order, the spinning stopped, and we were once again at the side of a road, one I'd never seen before. It looked to still be New Mexico, but it was warmer, and the vegetation was different. I looked around me, and saw another set of *descansos*, near a road sign that indicated we were about twenty miles from Carlsbad Caverns. We were in the southern part of the state, hundreds of miles from where we'd just been.

"Unbelievable," I said.

"Believe," he said. "It's energy, is all. People's love for people who passed away is real energy. We use that to travel."

"I do believe you," I said, looking deep into his eyes.

"Ready to move again?" he asked, hugging me tightly.

Again the ground fell away, and when we alighted, we were in a foot of snow beside roadside crosses, next to a field with six freezing, skin-and-bones cattle hunkered down against the wind.

"Come with me," Travis said as he jumped the fence to the field, and strode toward the cows. They looked at us with weary eyes, but didn't move away. They were too cold.

Travis laid his hands upon the weakest of the cows. Its sides fattened under his touch, its fur patched itself and thickened against the cold. When he'd finished with the animal, Travis focused his gaze on the land itself, and I watched in amazement as the snow began to melt beneath the bovines. The cows noticed, and stomped their feet and nodded their heads lightly, snorting their relief.

"I like burgers as much as the next guy, but I don't want them to suffer," he grumbled to me.

Travis tended to the others now, healing frostbitten legs and noses, fattening where starvation had set in.

"Okay," Travis said, after he'd finished. "Time to get you back to Grandma."

"They'll only be slaughtered and eaten in the end," I told him, feeling overwhelming sadness for the cows. "Why do you bother? Why can't you save them from that?"

"Everyone has a fate," he said. "Save them from the slaughter, and someone else starves. It's a strange universe we live in, Shane, equal parts creation and destruction, all of it in some crazy balance I don't understand either. Plus, death's not the end. Every living thing has a soul. They'll move on, to somewhere better."

"Why can't good stop evil completely?" I cried.

Travis held me around the waist with one hand, and stared into the distance. Again came the humming and again we moved through a twinkling storm. He did not answer me until we'd alighted once more, this time back at the memorial bench in the foothills near my house.

"I don't know," Travis told me, and I saw that his own eyes shimmered with tears. "I think sometimes that there's more than one creator. Or there's a Maker and a Destroyer. Like twins. Brothers."

I shivered, and Randy's face came to mind. I wondered if Travis thought the same. It seemed that Travis was considering his words more carefully, and at a deeper level, than he let on.

"Well, Shane, this is good-bye for now," he said. "I'm gonna find Buddy. If you don't feel me or see me for a bit, it's because that's where I am. Looking for him."

"So I'll see you again?"

He nodded, but winced, too.

"What if Victor tries to get me?" I asked.

"He won't. It's me he wants. If he thinks I'm not interested in you, he won't bother you. That's what I'm counting on."

"I need you."

"You'll be okay. But you should be extra careful about your ex-boyfriend anyway."

"Yeah. I know."

"So go, do your thing, get good grades, go to Kelsey's party. Oh—that reminds me. Shane, you need to act like they're right. I mean, about the brain injury."

I considered this. "Why?"

"To avoid losing anything else. Just act like they're

right, and stop talking about me to them."

I nodded, weakly, feeling sick and sad. He was serious about leaving me. He really believed he was causing me too many problems. I had to think of a way to change his mind.

"Okay," he said, like a magician on a stage, or an adult trying to distract a panicked child. "You ready to see something cool?"

I nodded stupidly.

"Ladies and gentlemen, here goes Travis's great vanishing act, part two. Ready?"

"No, actually," I said. "I'm not ready."

He ignored me again and—smiling in a silly, over-the-top way, like a circus performer—was almost immediately swallowed by a sudden, gusting tornado of golden light. As quickly as the swirl of air had come, it disappeared, taking Travis with it.

I felt his absence like a cold, hard punch in the gut.

eighteen

I spent the rest of the weekend sleeping and moping around, pretending to be "normal" again. On Monday my mother drove me to school because I was grounded from driving until further notice from my mother and the fleet of neurologists she was lining up to poke and prod me next week. Actually, she didn't think I was well enough to take my finals at all, but I convinced her to let me try. The school had said they would allow retakes if my performance proved to be inconsistent with the semester. I sat there in the passenger seat trying to act like I believed I had brain damage. It was degrading, the whole situation— faking brain injury, but also being left at the lower school drop-off area at Coronado Prep, a part of the campus most upper-school kids had intentionally managed to avoid since they'd turned sixteen.

But whatever misery I felt on the walk of shame from the lower school curb was nothing compared to the awkward, uncomfortable glances I started collecting from my classmates when I walked onto the campus of the upper school. Everywhere I went, I'd wave or smile at people who had just last week been my friends or acquaintances, only to have them respond tepidly and pityingly, whispering as I passed by, averting their eyes, giggling uncomfortably about me, and, now and then, giving me a hello that dripped with fear and suspicion. Dread filled my bones as I began to suspect everyone knew about my newfound "brain injury" and its resultant "insanity."

If I'd been naked in school, I could not have felt more self-conscious than I did now, as if everyone was watching me, mocking me in fascination, like I was some kind of local freak show attraction.

I was now an outcast.

I wasn't sure which of the two people who knew about my "hallucinations" had blabbed all over school, Kelsey or Logan, but given the way he'd treated me the night I broke up with him, my money was on the latter.

To clear my head, I walked across one of Coronado Prep's many landscaped quads, to the science complex. My father, who had gone to college back East, said the stately crimson brick buildings and towering trees on the grounds of my school reminded him of the way Ivy League schools looked in New England. It certainly required a lot of water to make anything in the desert look like a lush forest, and I figured a hefty chunk of our sizable tuition went to grounds maintenance and the water company.

I crunched across the snow with my head hung low. Discreetly, I opened a side door and slipped into the building, met by a soothing blast of heated air, in hopes of finding a warm place to hide before classes began. I couldn't handle the uncomfortable stares anymore. I just wanted to take my tests, and go home.

My first final exam that day was in Mr. Hedges's physics class. I was dying to ask him about parallel universes, and to tell him about what I'd experienced, but I didn't know how to bring it up. Anyway, there were too many people around to do it right now.

Kelsey was already in her seat. Logan was nowhere to be seen, and for this I was grateful.

"Hi," Kelsey said, looking guilty and sad.

I nodded in response, but didn't look up or say anything.

"It wasn't me," Kelsey said, knowing exactly what I was thinking and feeling. "So you can stop with the silent treatment."

I said nothing, and scrolled my laptop down in the review notes.

"It was Logan," she whispered. "Okay?"

"Yeah?" I mumbled. "And who told Logan, I wonder?"

"Fine. That was me. And I'm sorry I told him anything. I thought he'd be cool. I was really worried about you. I thought it would help. It was a mistake and I'm sorry."

I forced myself to fight back the tears.

"Shane, please don't be mad at me."

I looked at her now, and tried to remember that from her point of view, she was helping.

"Everyone hates me," I said. "They're all whispering."

"They don't *hate* you," she said. "They just—Logan made a Facebook group about you and invited everyone to join it. They've all seen it by now. It was everywhere yesterday. Everyone was texting me about it. I didn't want to upset you."

"A Facebook group about me?" I asked, horrified.

"He called it 'Let's All Help Shane Clark,' but it's actually all about how you're hallucinating and hearing voices, how you've lost it. He even found these photos he took on his camera-phone of you acting goofy, and put them up to make you look crazy."

"Why would he do that?" I asked, feeling very exposed and paranoid now.

"Because he's a jerk," she said.

"I broke up with him Friday night, after you left."

"That explains it then," she said.

Mr. Hedges came in, and the bell rang. We got our exams and remained quiet for the rest of the hour. I was so upset my hand shook when I gripped my pencil. I wasn't crazy. I wasn't losing my mind. I knew that what I'd experienced was real. Why couldn't anyone believe me?

I felt incredibly isolated, and miserable, but tried my best to focus on the test. The first question was about electricity and magnetism, and the irony of that fact did not escape me. Until that moment, these had been esoteric scientific topics that had little or no real bearing on my emotional life. Not anymore. Now I knew that human beings had only scraped the surface of what was out there, and what was possible. I knew, more than anyone else in this room, that electricity and magnetism governed more than the physical universe. They also ruled the spiritual universe. The physical and the spiritual were one and the same, but no one in my world seemed to realize this yet. This was what I thought about as I took my AP physics exam. It didn't matter that Travis wanted me to act normal; I was changed, and I'd never be "normal" again.

After I handed in my test, I asked Mr. Hedges if I could come by to talk to him about something later, and he said yes, giving me a copy of a handout that listed his office hours both at our school and at the university, where he kept a laboratory. I made a mental note to try to meet him at the university instead of here at Coronado Prep, so that no one would have any more reason to go around talking about me. I wanted to find Travis, and Mr. Hedges was the only person I could think of who might be able to help me do that.

The next period was study hall, which was held in the library. Kelsey was still trying to be nice to me. She didn't look down on me, or laugh at me, like some of the other kids seemed to be doing. She genuinely loved me, even if she did think I was losing my grip on reality.

Together, we gathered our things, and began to walk across the campus toward the library, which was better endowed than many college facilities. I braced against the cold wind, and tried to get Kelsey onto a new topic, away from my "injuries."

"What are you going to wear for the party?" I asked her, ignoring the group of girls who laughed at me from across a courtyard, and the other group of girls who gave me a fist pump and shouted, "Team Shane all the way!" while another group cried, "Team Logan!"

Great. I was a team now, all on my own.

"I'm not sure," Kelsey said, rolling her eyes at my detractors. "I was hoping maybe we could hit the mall next weekend, or sometime over break. I bet a new outfit would help you feel better."

"Yeah, sure," I said.

"You should try blue," she said, looking at me. "It'd be nice with your hair."

I tried to act normal, but I was overcome with a powerful unease as a flock of crows alighted on a branch in a tree above us, one of them swooping almost close enough to make me duck.

Kelsey didn't notice, and kept talking. "Or turquoise. It would really set off your eyes."

"Shape-shifter," I mused, looking up at the crow. It had green eyes, and watched me with a cold, hard intelligence. I hurried past it, no longer listening to Kelsey at all. Victor was here. He'd followed me. I needed to get inside.

"Shane? Did you hear me?" Kelsey asked as we arrived at the door to the library.

"Huh?" I asked, knowing that I must have looked panicked. "I'm sorry. What did you say?"

"I asked if you thought we should use white poinsettias on the porch or red ones."

"Red," I said, looking around nervously for the crow.

Kelsey was worried now. "Are you okay?" she asked me.

"Yeah," I lied. I tried to smile like the old Shane. I didn't know where she was anymore.

"Do you want me to call your mom?" she asked.

"What? No! Why?" I grabbed the handle to the door, and held it open for her to pass. She didn't budge.

205

"You don't seem like yourself. Maybe you should be home resting."

"I'm fine."

"I'm really sorry about all these idiots," Kelsey said, as a couple of kids passed by whispering about me. "It must feel terrible."

"I can handle it," I said, thinking that the snickering classmates were the least of my worries.

Kelsey and I walked across the library. To my dismay, I saw Logan here, too, with his calculus class. He sat with a group of kids and they all looked at me when I walked in, and burst out laughing.

"Morons," said Kelsey, putting a protective arm around me.

"What are they saying, you think?"

"Doesn't matter," she said.

I felt my eyes fill with tears. I tried to avoid everyone's gaze as Kelsey and I settled in at a table near the windows that faced out onto the expansive playing fields.

"Are you still talking to him?"

"Who?"

"Travis," she said.

I shrugged and avoided looking at her. I didn't want to talk about it.

"Shane." Still staring. "What are you hiding? You won't even look at me."

I finally met her eyes, and sighed, hoping she'd notice how weary and unhappy she was making me.

"I'm not talking to him anymore," I said. "Happy?"

She frowned. "I'm not happy, no. I think it's the best thing for you, but I know you think you care about him."

I turned my eyes to the playing fields once more, hoping to calm my brain down enough to slip into a cozy denial, but this was not to be, because tied to one of the trees was a small black dog.

"Buddy!" I cried.

The rope was long and red, and stood out crisply against the white snow, as did the dog. My dog.

"Omigod," I said, under my breath. My pulse did that thing it was getting so good at now, and began to hammer away inside of me.

Kelsey looked outside where I was looking, and asked, "Why is your dog on the playing field, Shane?" From her tone of voice, she seemed to think I'd put him there.

"I don't know," I said.

I scanned the field, looking for Travis. But I saw nothing. Just Buddy, the red rope, the trees, and the otherwise vacant snowy fields. Buddy, being his usual self and appearing unharmed, tugged at the rope and yapped at the flock of crows flying overhead.

Soon, the rope came loose from the tree, and Buddy got his wish for freedom. He scampered like a lunatic across the field, chasing the crows straight toward the road. The good news was that the road was far enough away that it would take Buddy a minute or two to get there. The bad news was that Buddy was inexplicably drawn to busy streets, and seemed to think that it was a Chihuahua's macho duty in life to challenge moving cars to a duel, confident that he would always win. Given that he was roughly the same color as the blacktop, I was always rescuing him from being run over.

"Oh, no," I said, in a panic.

Before I knew what I was doing, I was up out of my seat, shrugging back into my jacket and backpack, hightailing it toward the door, against every school rule, and with the eyes of a couple dozen newly minted enemies upon me.

"Shane!" cried Kelsey. "Get back here!"

I ignored her, and sprinted out the door, down the steps, and around the building, toward the playing fields. I ran and ran, and soon saw Buddy tripping along happily toward the road.

"Buddy!" I screamed, elated to see him again, but terrified he'd get hit by a car. "Stop! Stop!"

As usual, he turned to acknowledge that he'd heard my voice and command, and then quickly ignored me and kept running.

"No! Bad dog! Stay!"

Buddy stopped, but only to sniff a tumbleweed and pee on it. Then he was off and trotting again.

"Stop right now!" I shrieked, sprinting faster. The cold air made me cough, but I kept running. When I got to within ten feet of him, Buddy seemed to realize that resistance was futile at last. He curled his body toward me, simpering, and dropped to his back, apologetic.

"Bad dog!" I said again as I reached him.

Buddy wagged his tail and flattened his ears against his head to let me know he meant it.

I scooped him up into my arms, and kissed him. "You bad, stupid, crazy little dog!" I kissed him again. "What is wrong with you?"

Buddy licked my chin, as though "loving Shane" was the correct answer. Perhaps it was.

"Where have you been?"

I was so happy to have him back, I almost couldn't stand it. I cried and laughed, and snuggled and cuddled him. I was so involved with this emotional reunion that I almost didn't notice Travis standing between a couple of evergreens at the far end of the field, watching. I was about to run to him, to ask him about Buddy and to thank him, but he shook his head, a somber and apologetic look in his eyes, and held a hand out to stop me.

I stopped, and stared in horror as he mouthed, "I love you," and waved good-bye.

"No!" I screamed. I started running toward him. Devastatingly, he took a few paces back and away from me, toward a statue on the grounds that had been erected in memory of Coronado Prep's founder.

A memorial.

Just like that, in a split second of swirling air, he was gone.

"No!" I sobbed, falling to my knees in the snow, sobbing because I knew what that look had meant. He was gone. He would never be back. I'd never smell him, touch him, or see him again. Overhead, high up in a tree, a crow let out a call that sounded very much like laughter.

I stayed hunched there, crying hysterically with Buddy in my lap, for a few minutes, until I heard footsteps coming up behind me. When I looked up, I saw the headmaster of the school barreling down on me, flanked by the school librarian and Kelsey.

"There she is," Kelsey said, fear in her voice.

"Miss Clark," said the headmaster. "Is everything all right?"

"No!" I cried, trying to see the bird in the tree, feeling more miserable than I'd felt in all my life. "Everything's not okay. Everything's over."

"I think you should call her mom," said my best friend. "Shane had an accident, and she might have hit her head. She doesn't mean any of this."

Kelsey ran to me, and hugged me, telling me everything was going to be fine. I couldn't stop crying.

"Come on, now," she said. "Let's get you to the nurse."

On feet and legs numb with cold and grief, I staggered upright, holding Buddy like a treasure I didn't want anyone to take from me, and I stumbled along with them, looking every bit like the mental patient they were all certain, at last, that I was.

nineteen

After visiting a brain doctor that afternoon, I was told all looked good and I was allowed to return to school for the rest of the week to finish my exams. I forced myself through the motions of my old life, and tried to remember that I had been happy and productive before I met Travis. Somehow, I told myself, I would not be a girl who fell apart because she lost a guy; not even one as remarkable as Travis. At night I slept and hoped he'd come to me, but he did not. Travis, it seemed, was making good on his promise to leave me alone, and as the days passed, I began to understand that he might have been right. Life would never be the same, and I'd always know that there was more out there, but at least I wasn't afraid anymore, as I had been before. I realized that ever since meeting Travis, life had changed forever, with no way back. It had been loving, what he did, abandoning me. This, I knew. It did not make his absence any easier, but it made the sadness easier to endure—that somewhere out there he still existed, and he still loved me.

I went home with Kelsey after finals that Friday afternoon, with my mother's permission, to help her prepare for her holiday party. We both wondered whether people would still come, knowing that she was my friend and I was the school pariah, but she, a good friend in spite of it all, assured me that she would rather be my friend than be popular, which I am certain was supposed to sound a lot nicer than it actually did.

Kelsey lived in the university area in the center of town, in a neighborhood known as Ridgecrest. I was sorely tempted to run off to the university to talk to Mr. Hedges, but Kelsey would absolutely have told my mother if I did anything weird anymore. I had to give the total illusion of being a normal girl again.

Her house was a lot older than mine, but it had a charm and warmth that my house—both my houses, really, if you counted my dad's, which I saw so infrequently it didn't count—lacked. It was located on a tree-lined street with a grassy median, was white stucco with a red tile roof, and had turquoise trim on the shutters, doors, and windows. While in our High Desert neighborhood it was

213

against the rules to have grass or anything that required a lot of water to grow, there were no such regulations here, and the front yard had a nice lawn.

Kelsey's parents were home when we got there. They were still almost sickeningly in love, after more than thirty years of marriage, and I envied Kelsey for that. Most of my memories of my parents together were of them fighting. I envied Kelsey's parents for other reasons, too. They were artsy; and calm, relaxed people; and seemed genuinely grounded, balanced, and interested in anything you had to say. They didn't hover and act like military interrogators the way my mom sometimes did; they didn't mope around looking guilty for taking a single second for their own needs and fun. Kelsey's parents, luckily enough for her, had lives of their own, and those lives seemed rich, rewarding, and full of interesting people.

Kelsey had a couple of younger brothers, but her parents had the nanny over to watch them in the nursery wing of the sprawling one-story house, so they wouldn't get in our way. Kelsey had her own wing, adjacent to it, separated from the younger boys by a large laundry room and a music room that housed a baby grand piano, a drum set, guitars, and all sorts of other cool stuff. Kelsey's room itself wasn't nearly as large as mine, but it was more interesting in some ways because it had a loft for a bed, accessible by a ladder and descendible by a circular slide.

This had been more fun, of course, when we were a little younger, but we still managed to make good use of it. The room was decorated in muted earth tones, and had real art on the walls. It was elegant, but still a teenager's room, and at the moment we had music blasting.

Our friend Lindsey was there, too, having followed us from school in her own car, and having said nothing about me now being an outcast. We'd brought our dresses and collective makeup, shoes, and accessories. And I was doing a very convincing job of telling them I was getting better from the accident, and they were more than happy to play along. We seemed, in most ways, to be the way we might have been a month ago. A tray of snacks, brought in by the guest chef Kelsey's parents had hired to cater the party that night, sat basically untouched on Kelsey's desk. I wondered, silently, which dress Travis would have preferred on me, and bit my tongue against the powerful urge to tell my friends all about him.

In the end, I'd settled on a classic, elegant black sleeveless dress, taffeta, with a fitted bodice and a flared skirt that ended at the knee, with a playful pink sash around the waist, twisted into a bow in the back. It was flirty and fun.

"Forget about Logan, the jerk," Lindsey told me, not realizing my depression had nothing to do with having broken up with Logan.

215

"Serious jerk," Kelsey agreed. "After all you've been through, for him to pull this? Ugh. I knew there was a reason I didn't like that guy."

We all changed into our dresses together, and adjusted one another's buttons and zippers. Then we took turns doing our makeup at the mirror over Kelsey's dresser, helping one another. I went light on the eyes, but Lindsey set me straight. Her mother was an actress in the theater in town, and so she knew about stage makeup.

"A party," she told us, "is a performance. The lights will be low, and you deserve to have eyes that pop."

She lined my eyes in black all the way around, and stuck fake lashes to my top lids. It felt awkward and uncomfortable, but made my eyes look twice as big as ever. I wore my hair mostly down, with a few front layers pinned up, and my friends helped me set it with hot rollers so that it cascaded in pretty waves. Kelsey wore a sky-blue silk dress that set off her eyes beautifully, and Lindsey helped her pile her hair up in an elegant twist. Lindsey wore a hot-orange dress that set off her skin tone, and she put sparkly flower barrettes in her kinky hair. In the end, we all looked fabulous, and we knew it. When we went to the dining room to show the grown-ups, Kelsey's parents looked completely surprised and overjoyed.

"You kids look like you just stepped off an episode of *The Real World*," said Kelsey's mom. We tried not to be too annoyed at the attempt to be cool. Instead, we just said thanks.

Soon enough, the doorbell rang and rang again and again as more kids came, which was good because it meant Kelsey's reputation had not been tarnished for having known me. I began to let my guard down. I ate mushroom puff pastries, and drank root beer, and was pulled into a dance.

Kelsey and I went into the kitchen to tell her mom we needed more sodas, and she asked that we quickly take a couple of bags of trash out to the black barrel in the alley behind the house. We took the bags and headed outside, giggling about the success of the party.

twenty

Kelsey lifted the lid of the trash barrel, and I hurled the green, bulging bags of noxious garbage into it. She'd just slammed it shut and turned with me to go back to the house when I first sensed, and then saw, a person standing at the gate to the yard, in the shadows, blocking our way. Whoever it was wore a long, dark hooded robe, monastic, that concealed their face. Kelsey hadn't looked up yet and was still chattering on to me about the boy she had a crush on. I gripped her arm to stop her.

"Ow," she said, annoyed, trying to break free. I guess I'd grabbed her a little harder than I meant to. My pounding heart was in my throat and I could barely find the air to speak.

"There's someone there," I whispered, pointing.

Kelsey's eyes followed the line of my finger, and settled on the hooded figure. She stood stock-still, surprised but not yet afraid, perhaps because she did not yet know the sorts of things that existed in our universe, and what they were capable of doing.

"Probably homeless," she whispered back as she turned discreetly to walk in the opposite direction, pulling me with her. "We've been having a problem with that lately around here. Come on."

I walked with her, knowing she intended to simply double back around the block and go in through the front door, but I did not share her conviction that this was a homeless person we simply needed to leave be. My gut instinct told me it was something else, and every hair on my body rose up in terror. My mouth was dry, and my footsteps fell as daintily as I could make them, as quietly as they could go. I hoped we hadn't been noticed, but at a deeper level I knew—with a sick feeling—that we'd not only been spotted, we had been watched closely.

"My mom's been talking about moving because the neighborhood's deteriorating," Kelsey whispered, looping her arm through mine. "She says I'm going to have to grow up streetwise if we stay near the university, and—"

Kelsey stopped talking abruptly, because two additional hooded figures stepped out of the shadows in front of us now, blocking our way. They made no noise, and seemed to float ever so slightly above the earth. Ghostlike, I thought.

"What the—," Kelsey said. She spun to look behind us, and screamed. I turned to see what had caused this, and saw four hooded figures behind us. Spinning once more, I saw that the two who had been in front of us were now joined by two others. There were eight hooded men in all, moving silently, eerily toward us in the darkness of the narrow alley.

"Just stay calm," I said. "No sudden moves."

"Mom!" Kelsey shrieked, ignoring my advice. "Mom! Help! Somebody help us!"

The shadows rushed us then, soundlessly, surrounded us, and I could see that while some of them were solid and visible at night, others were not. It appeared to be a mixture of the living and the dead.

"Help!" screamed Kelsey, but I was unable to choke out a single sound, for I had noticed, upon trying to see the faces of the hooded figures, that one of them had familiar red eyes glowing out at me. I became numb with fear.

Two enormous figures, whatever they were, picked us up from the ground, one hoisting me effortlessly over his shoulder and the other stuffing Kelsey under his arm as though she were light as a rolled-up newspaper. Surrounded protectively by the rest of the group, as though this had all been skillfully choreographed long before, they carried us away, both of us instinctively kicking and struggling pathetically. The creatures moved swiftly, smoothly, as though they were on wheels and with nearly superhuman speed, first to the end of the alley, and then around a corner, and finally to an unlit nearby park. They flitted from one dark shadow to the next, the sheer fluid flowingness of their motions keeping them undetected by anyone who might have been passing by. I started to scream, but the creature who held me clamped his cold fist like a hard, dead stone over my mouth.

"I wouldn't do that if I were you," he said with a bit of a snarl, in a voice that sounded more monster than human.

Kelsey continued to scream as we approached a large, dark SUV. The creature holding her took a handkerchief from his pocket and held it hard and fast over Kelsey's nose and mouth as she struggled. I watched in horror as she appeared to suffocate and pass out, her arms and legs splaying limply in every direction.

"No!" I tried to scream, but it came out muffled through the hand over my mouth. One of them was on top of me then, binding my wrists and ankles with rope and duct tape. They tied Kelsey up in the same way even though she wasn't conscious. One of them held a cloth like the one they'd used on Kelsey, and pressed it over my nose and mouth. I breathed in a noxious poison and felt woozy, sick, lost, and dizzy. They lifted me up, and tossed me into the cargo area in the back of the vehicle. I landed with a whump that I knew should have hurt, but I couldn't feel my body anymore. The world grew fuzzier, and farther away, quieter, more echoing and vague. The hooded figures receded, and I was fading, fading, and the doors were slamming shut, and the car was starting, and then . . . nothing.

twenty-one

When I came to, I didn't know how much time had passed since I blacked out in the back of the SUV. I found myself still tied up, on a bed in a half-dark room. I was panicked because my mind went to the worst possible place it could go. I prayed that nothing horrible had happened to me, that I hadn't been raped. I prayed for Travis to find me. I prayed that Kelsey was unharmed.

I lifted my head, which pounded as though my brain were swelling in pulsating rhythm, and saw that my dress and stockings seemed to still be intact. My mouth was dry, and I tried to move my hands but they were bound behind my back. My shoulders and neck ached from the awkward position. *Travis,* I thought, *where are you? Help me.*

I struggled to sit up, and turned my head this way and that, searching for Kelsey. But all I saw was a very small, very dingy room, with a bed and a dresser and a chair that appeared to be falling apart. There was a smell of mildew and stale cigarette smoke, and possibly a clogged toilet somewhere. It was rank, rancid, disgusting. A single naked bulb dangled from a frayed cord in the ceiling above me, buzzing on and off at random intervals, as though there was a storm somewhere. There were curtains on the windows, but they were open and I could see that the sun was either just coming up, or just going down. A closer look revealed them to be stained children's sheets, with cartoon characters on them. My pulse raced. I had seen these sheets before.

I wriggled and grunted, trapped and desperate. All I could think about was getting out of here. How could I do it? I opened my mouth to cry out, but thought better of it. What if the only people—or things—who would be here to hear my cry were bad? What if my scream brought nothing but those hooded figures and more poison? I clamped my jaw shut, and began to look for something, anything, to use as a tool to free myself. Something sharp, maybe, to cut the bonds. That was when I noticed the man standing in the shadows near the closed door. He was tall and lean and his eyes, shiny in the dark, were watching me. I saw a red ember just below them. It grew brighter for a moment, then dimmed again. Someone was in the room with me, and he was smoking.

I backed instinctively away from the figure, toward the rotten plywood headboard of the creaking bed. This only caused whomever it was to laugh to himself. I recognized that voice, that low smooth tenor, that unsympathetic guffaw.

"Good morning, sunshine," he said, as he stepped out of the shadows. The pale glow of the light made his skin glow with a red hue, but the rest was as it had been the last time I'd seen him, at school. Khaki pants, an Izod sweater with a button-down shirt beneath it.

"Logan?" I asked, confused. "What are you doing here? What's going on?"

"Shane, Shane, Shane," he said, sucking the ember bright orange again. In the light from the end of the cigarette, I could see his eyes crinkle in a smile—but it was a smile without a hint of kindness. I had never seen him smoke before, and he seemed like a completely different boy from the one I used to date. "Nice to see you again, baby."

"Don't call me baby," I spat.

This seemed to excite him, and he chuckled some more, walking slowly back and forth at the foot of the bed, looking at me with eyes that seemed to have a supernatural yellow glow to them.

"Why not, baby? Don't you like it? You never complained when I called you baby before, or when I touched you."

He came closer, and made as if to touch me now.

"Get away from me."

He laughed. "Oh, if only it were that simple," he said.

"What are you going to do to me?" I asked him.

He came close now, and touched my hair, my cheek. It felt disgusting, filthy, terrifying. "What am I going to do to you?" he repeated thoughtfully. "Now there's a good question, baby."

He sighed deeply and sat next to me on the bed. How could something so attractive be so evil? I thought. Looking at him was something like looking at a lion close up at the zoo. You recognized the majestic beauty of the thing, but you also realized it could easily slice you in two and eat you for breakfast.

"What did you do to Kelsey?" I asked.

"She'll be here as soon as she wakes up. We have her in the next room. I wanted to have a moment to chat with you alone first."

"What did you do to us, while we were unconscious?"

"Don't worry. Much as I would have liked it, I didn't defile you. No one did. We were under orders not to."

"From who?"

"My new mentor," he said. "You might not have

226

understood what I meant about power and life and death, but he does. He's smart, unlike some people."

At that moment, the door opened, and a flood of light poured in from the dank hallway. It looked like we were in an old trailer of some kind. The trailer from the dream, I realized. Victor's house.

In the doorway, I saw two men standing on either side of Kelsey, who looked like she'd been roughed up a bit. A third man I could not quite see stood behind them.

"Shane!" she cried when she saw me. "Are you okay?"

"I'm fine," I told her. "Are you?"

"I'm okay."

"Shut up, please," said a familiar, sickening voice, low and rumbly, completely psychotic. "You're giving me a headache."

Victor.

The two men came into the room, and dumped Kelsey on the bed. Victor followed, as ugly and hideous as he'd been in the dreams. He was whole again now, and wickedly excited to see me.

"Do you have any idea how sick this guy is?" I asked Logan. "What are you doing? He wouldn't hesitate to kill you, too."

Victor laughed at my panic. Logan looked at him as though requesting permission to answer me, and Victor cut him down with a curt shake of his head. With Kelsey squirming on the bed next to me, the other two men retreated to the wall near the window, to stand guard. I noticed now that Logan had his hunting knife in his waistband. Kelsey and I scooted as close to each other as we could, not that this was going to help in the event that we were stabbed.

"Here is the short version of the story for you, Shane," said Victor, pacing nervously back and forth, in a way that very much reminded me of the coyote he sometimes materialized as. "Travis loves you. I hate Travis. The best way I can think of to hurt Travis is to hurt the one he loves."

"He's gone from my life now!" I cried. "He said so himself. He knew you'd do this, so he and I aren't together anymore."

Victor cut me off, a violent rage boiling in his eyes.

"Silence!" he roared, stalking in a strange way, shifting shape before our very eyes. His shoulders grew hunched, and his arms became thinner, and longer, and the bones made a terrible din of crunching and crackling, as he became a coyote. Even so, he was able to keep talking, through his coyote's mouth, the voice deep and horrible now, snarling and phlegmy.

"I'm a smart man," he said. "You might not guess that to see this house, but I *am* smart. If I hurt you—and I will, don't you doubt it—he'll come for you. It don't matter what he promised. He's weak. He'll come. And when he does, he'll break a rule. I'll make sure of it. He'll be tempted, and in that temptation, he'll mess up. They think they're better 'n me, just like that bitch mama of theirs, but they're not. Him and Randy, they're just like me."

"They're nothing like you!" I screamed, as Kelsey whimpered next to me.

My outburst infuriated Victor. He shape-shifted again. I heard the bones of his body as they crunched and grew and shrank and reformed in the shape of something I can only describe as a demon, hairless and spiny, with a long, barbed tail. The voice, when it came, was even worse now than it had been before.

"Here," he growled. "It'll all end right here, in this room, but not without a little bit of fun first."

I didn't ask anything more, because I didn't like the look of the way he licked his chops and his red eyes glowed at us.

"Logan here is my friend. I found him the night you walked with him. His soul called out to me, and I answered its call. There are some among you who seek to be associated with my kind. They reach out in their own ways, through their own magic, and I was lucky enough to find him just in time to make this beautiful arrangement we have here happen. The Maker works in mysterious ways."

"The Maker had nothing to do with you, or any of this!" I raged. "You're disgusting!"

Victor came in close then, and kissed me on the lips. I resisted, and spit the sticky, putrid taste off of me when he was done. Kelsey somehow curled her legs into her chest and unleashed them with a stunning blow to Victor's chin, knocking him down, to protect me.

Victor rose up, furious, with bright red blood dripping from his lower lip, and unsheathed a knife with slow, cold deliberation and a devilish smile. The blade, engraved with snaking, moving lettering, gleamed.

"You shouldn't have done that, little best friend," he told her. "You do realize you're the disposable one here, don't you, blondie?"

"No!" I screamed, as he came close to her and, grabbing her hair in his free hand, yanked her head back and held the blade to her throat. "She was only trying to help me! Take me. Not her. She hasn't done anything to you."

"It's true, your brave cowboy won't come for Kelsey," Victor hissed in her face, spittle dripping from his lips. "Pretty as you are, Kelsey, delicious as you look, Travis don't care about *you*. No boy does. And that hurts you, don't it? I see what Shane can't. You're jealous of her."

Kelsey's face was a messy mix of fear and pain. Suddenly, I understood why someone like Victor might choose to prey upon his enemy's loved ones rather than the enemy himself. It was because good people suffered more for others than for themselves, and more than I wanted to save myself, I wanted to help Kelsey.

Victor laughed in her face as he pointed to me with his clawed hand. "It's her he wants. I could cut you right here, right now, and it wouldn't make a bit of difference to my plan."

"Please don't," she stammered, trembling.

Victor clearly got off on watching her squirm, just as Logan had enjoyed watching the jackrabbit squirm. Then, he abruptly sheathed the blade once more, and stood up to face me with a wild grin.

"I'll wait to take care of your friend—later, after you've gone to sleep. You, pathetically, *love* your little *friend*. Pity. I wouldn't want you so traumatized that you won't be of help when he finally get here."

With that, he produced the handkerchief, and once more put it over my nose and mouth, as Kelsey screamed. The world faded, and then I was gone, falling into a deep, dark, blank, horrible sleep.

twenty-two

I woke up feeling nauseous, to the sound of a punishing rain on a metal roof. The cartoon curtains in the rancid bedroom where I was still held captive were drawn. I could tell it was daytime, albeit a dreary, gray day that felt hopeless and suffocating. I was still on the bed, as I was the last time I came to, and my wrists and ankles were still bound tightly. It felt as though I had no circulation in my hands and feet anymore. I was thirsty, and hungry, and I needed to pee. Kelsey was gone again, and I was alone in the room now. I struggled to maneuver myself to the edge of the bed, and wriggled to get myself to my feet. My high-heeled pumps were nowhere to be seen, and the carpet felt like a dry, hard Brillo pad under my feet. I looked about me wildly, hoping to find my phone. My purse. But none of it was here. I wondered what my mother thought. There must have been people out looking for us by then. I wondered how long I'd been unconscious, what day it was. I held a small flame of hope in my heart that he might somehow find me here.

I tried a few pathetic hops, with the aim of getting myself to the dresser so that I could attempt to saw the bindings off my wrists with its lopsided edge—but all I managed to do was fall, with a loud whump, to the floor. It was filthy, with dead cockroaches on it and, to my horror, a few live ones, too. I screamed.

I heard footsteps coming—or, I should say, I felt them. I braced myself in dread. I heard the door open, a person breathing and moving slowly, looking for me. From where they stood, they would not have been able to see me because of the position of the bed.

"Come out, come out, wherever you are," called Victor's disgusting voice, in sinister imitation of a child's game.

I held my breath, hoping irrationally that he couldn't find me if I just stopped breathing.

"Peekaboo," he said next, as I saw his head round the edge of the bed, smiling horribly, viciously. "I see you. . . ."

With one unfathomably strong hand, the demon picked me up off the floor and dumped me back onto the bed. I screamed as loudly as I could. Suddenly a moving blur came flying across the room from the doorway and tackled Victor. They began to wrestle.

"Travis!" I cried, as I recognized him.

I watched in horror as they pummeled each other. Travis moved with great skill, however—and was stronger and more agile than Victor. In fact, Travis seemed to handle Victor as though he were some sort of enormous livestock. Soon, Travis had rope out, and was literally hogtying the demon's limbs. He wrapped the rope around Victor's head, and tied that up, too. Victor could not move, other than to struggle against the bindings. They were already coming loose, however, and I knew we didn't have much time before he'd be back up.

"He's getting out!" I cried.

"Shh," Travis said, finger to his lips.

"You shouldn't have come!" I cried. "He's going to hurt you!"

"Quiet," he commanded.

He sawed at my bindings with a Swiss Army knife until they popped, and a wave of blood flowed from my arms to my fingertips in a painful but refreshing tingle. He repeated this process with my ankles.

"Thank God you're here," I breathed into his neck.

"Shh, not now." He lifted me onto his shoulder as though I weighed nothing, and sprinted from the room, down a dank and narrow hallway, and out the front door.

Running with superhuman strength and speed, he hauled me across the fallow, frozen wasteland outside, and set me gently in the bottom of a dry irrigation ditch, out of sight from the trailer.

Speaking in a firm voice, he said, "Stay down. Don't move. Don't scream. No noise. I'm going back for Kelsey. Wait here."

"He said he was going to kill her," I told him.

Travis rushed to my side, and put his face, deadly serious, directly in front of mine. "I told you to be absolutely quiet. I need your cooperation. Now. Life or death, Shane. Please."

I did as he said, my heart thundering in my chest. I began to shiver, and my shoeless feet began to freeze. I wanted to peek up and get a sense of where I was, but I knew better than to defy his command right now. Right now, he knew more than I did.

Travis returned a few minutes later, with Kelsey on his shoulder. She was as stunned and terrified as I was.

Travis crouched next to us. "You guys ready to get out of here?"

We nodded vigorously.

"Yeah, me, too. I need to get you to the *descansos*, and then we can transport you home. I'll deal with Victor after that."

We crouched with him. Travis whistled, and Scooter,

the horse he'd ridden the first day I met him, came gal-
loping out of the nothingness. Travis threw us one at a
time onto his back, and was about to come up after us
when we heard the sound of a motor in the near distance.
An all-terrain vehicle was bearing down upon us over a
nearby hill, driven by none other than Logan. Victor, back
in human form, stood triumphantly behind him, like an
overseer, pointing his finger to where we were. They were
gaining on us quickly. Travis, his eyes betraying courage
and lightning-quick plotting, slapped Scooter's hip and
said, "Yah, go! To the *descansos*!"

Scooter took off, without him, racing across the desert
through the rain, in the direction of Highway 550 and
Travis's and Randy's *descansos*. I craned my neck in a panic,
trying to see Travis, and saw Logan and Victor speeding
straight toward him. I screamed, but to my astonishment,
Travis jumped up and over the ATV, landing on the other
side of it. Logan spun the vehicle around, aimed it at
Travis again, and charged while Victor laughed mania-
cally. Missing him a second time, Victor seemed to think
up a new plan. He spoke into Logan's ear, and instead of
going after Travis again, Logan turned with a filthy smile
on his face, and began to chase after *us*.

Scooter seemed to perceive this, because he hastened
his pace, and Kelsey and I held on to his mane for dear life.
But his speed was no match for the ATV, and before we

knew what was happening, Logan was revving his engine right next to us, trying to ram the vehicle into Scooter's side and legs as Victor licked his chops at us like a hungry dog. The horse—in revenant form, I presumed—dodged, and stopped in his tracks to rear up, whinnying with a crazed look in his wide-set eyes. Victor placed a hand on Logan's shoulder. Logan stopped the ATV suddenly, and then Victor rose up even taller, with a large electric crossbow and arrow. Victor aimed the hideous weapon at the horse.

"No!" I screamed, but the arrow made a whizzing sound, zipping through the air with astonishing speed and accuracy, landing squarely in Scooter's side, toppling him instantly. Kelsey and I were thrown from the horse several yards. I looked back, horrified and heartbroken, and saw the horse struggling on his side, squealing in pain. I knew he was already dead, a ghost horse, a revenant like Travis, and I wondered whether the same rules applied to the horse that applied to him. If Travis were to allow himself to be killed again, in revenant form, he would be instantly condemned to the Underworld.

"Scooter! No!" I cried, hurrying to his side to try to help him. But it was too late. When I got to him, he had already stopped breathing, his eyes glazed over by death.

Logan hopped off the ATV and ran over to watch the dead horse with a fascinated look on his face.

"Did you see that?" he asked me, pleased with himself, as though we were still friends. "The way his soul left his body? Did you see that?" His eyes were manic, excited with his own power and bloodlust.

Travis came running toward us now, a look of sheer fury and sadness on his face as he spotted Scooter downed, and understood he was gone. Victor, upon seeing Travis coming closer, suddenly lunged from the ATV for me. He zipped through the air effortlessly and pinned my back against his chest, holding Logan's massive hunting knife to my throat. Logan watched Victor with a look of surprise, as though he hadn't actually counted on the demon being capable of killing people, and realized now that Victor would do it. Logan was so naive.

"Victor, yo man!" Logan called out. "What are you doing?"

"Shut. Up," Victor hissed at my former boyfriend.

"Whoa, you said we were gonna scare 'em, shake 'em up a little, not—"

"Silence!" Victor commanded with a damning look, sinking the blade just a bit into my skin. Then Victor spun us around so that we both faced Travis. I tried to find air, but I couldn't breathe.

Travis slowed to a walk, confusion and agony washing over his face as he tried to figure out what to do next.

"Shane!" screamed Kelsey hysterically.

"Just stay back," Travis instructed her. "Get back, stay away."

She did as he told her, and though I couldn't see her anymore, I could hear her muttering prayers to herself, and whimpering, crying.

"Sometimes, Logan, as y'already know, it's just not enough to scare 'em," Victor said, his tone logical and cold in my ear. I felt his lips move excitedly against my skin, and realized that to him this was a form of intimacy. "You've killed a lot of animals, and now, you gotta admit, Logan, it's just not enough of a rush no more. Consider this your first real lesson from your new mentor. Logan? Are you listening?"

I heard Logan's voice quake as he answered, "Yes, sir."

"Come," said Victor to him. "Take the knife. You hold her now."

There was a pause.

"What did I just say?" roared Victor. "Either you do as I tell you, Logan, or you go with her."

Logan came and took Victor's place holding me captive. Travis still watched, doing nothing.

"Good," said Victor. "She's been nothin' but a little bitch to you, Logan. Now's your chance to make her pay."

"Sir," said Logan uncertainly. I could feel him trembling.

"Let her go, Logan," said Travis, coming closer, slowly.

"You don't want to do this."

Victor answered for Logan. "Oh, that's where you're wrong, cowboy. He *does*. He does wanna do this."

"Well, forgive me, Victor," Travis said sarcastically. "I wouldn't have a clue what it's like to want to hurt another human being. Especially Shane."

"Is that right?" asked Victor in a slippery tone. "That's not what a little birdie told me. From what I understand, you're no superhero, Travis. After all, wasn't it you, the little brother, who told your big brother to pull the trigger on me? Ain't you the one who actually made it happen? Isn't that knowledge what keeps you up at night? Ain't that really why you stick by Randy, no matter how much he screws up? Because you know whose fault it really was that I died."

Travis's face dropped.

"That's what I thought," Victor sneered. "Yeah. You know your true potential, Travis. You know you're no different from me. Or Logan. Ain't that right? It's not as simple as you make it out to be, cowboy. It's not just good guys and bad guys, is it? Shades of freakin' gray."

"Let her go. She didn't do anything to you," Travis demanded of Logan.

"Oh, but you're wrong," Logan said, seeming to change now, pushing the blade into my neck. The pain was sharp, red and achy, like a supreme paper cut. I gulped for air like a fish out of water. Logan continued, "She *dumped* me. For you. No one dumps me."

"That's it," Victor said to Logan. "Good boy. Make her pay."

"Shane!" Kelsey shrieked.

Victor spoke again. "Imagine how good it'd feel, Logan, to finish her now, in front of the man she left you for. You'd see them both suffer. And they'd both lose their souls."

"The only soul that would be lost if you killed Shane would be your own, Logan," Travis said. "Think hard about this. This isn't who you really are."

Then, before I could understand what was happening, Travis lunged through the air, and attacked Logan. Somehow, in an instant, the knife went flying, and I was freed, and I stood for a moment, trying to figure out whether I could help Travis.

"Run, Shane, Kelsey, go!" Travis shouted as he wrestled with Logan quite violently. Victor, oddly, just watched, smiling. He probably was waiting for Travis to kill Logan, or to mess up in some other way. After all, that was the goal of all of this, to back Travis into a corner.

Travis called out to us, "Get to the *descansos*! Go!"

I did as he told me, grabbing Kelsey's hand and pulling her along with me. I ran, as fast as I could in stocking feet that were frozen all the way through, over rocks, ice, and cactus. Like a coward, I ran.

With Kelsey limping along beside me, I ran for the highway, as every ounce of energy I had was channeled into the simple act of survival. My breath came ragged, my chest heaved with the effort, and I feared for Travis, but I did not look back and I did not stop. Behind me was death. Life lay ahead.

We made it over the top of the rise, and I pointed us in the direction of the two white crosses on the side of the road. We began to slip and slide down the scrubby hill. I breathed a little. We were almost there.

Suddenly I felt a hand wrap around my wet, matted hair, yanking forcefully. My head was jerked so violently I saw stars, and I stumbled, and fell with a sickening crunch as the rocks smashed into my nearly bare kneecaps. I rolled my eyes up, as my head was tilted vigorously backward, at such a sharp angle that I felt the bones in my neck begin to crack. The back of my head was flush up against the top of my back now, and a fiery pain seared my spine all the way down. From this loathsome angle I could see Victor's face grinning down at me madly, as he held me powerfully in his unwavering grip. He was still in human form. His nose bled, his lips were swollen and split, and his eyes were blackened from being beaten. He had the wickedly happy look of a man who was only getting started.

I saw Travis stumbling up from behind, also badly

battered. In the distance, I saw Logan tied up on the ground like a calf. I had only enough time to connect my eyes with Travis's before the knife was out, flashing in Victor's hand as he raised it high above him.

"Here's how it's done, Logan!" cried Victor, in a voice so loud it boomed.

Travis's eyes lost their usual careful composure, filled instead with a look of pure dismay and horror that I had never seen on him, and could not imagine seeing on him except that here it was, staring down at me with complete despair.

Victor's hand slashed downward through the air in front of my face, the handle of the hunting knife held fast and tight in his fist. So, so fast the terrible thing happened, so fast that experiencing it felt like remembering it. There was only enough time to register that the knife had been sunk deep into my throat, a brief and horrifying moment to experience it sawing back and forth, as I felt the syrupy warm wetness gushing out of my neck with alarming volume and speed, before everything became dark, and cold, and still.

A complete and holy silence washed over me, and molded itself into a hard, quick shell, over everything I was and had ever been. I was, suddenly, nothing, and that brought its own brand of fear, a new terror of lostness I could not name; it was worse than the horrific, mind-boggling pain that had preceded it. Lamentably, I understood, the girl I had been no longer existed. I had no body. No breath. No heartbeat. No vision. No sense of smell. No hearing. No future. Would there be no Travis? But just as fast as I felt fear, it faded into nothing. Just nothing. I had nothing. I was nothing, and as nothing, frozen in a thick, infinite web, woven of endless nothingness, I felt, unsurprisingly, nothing at all.

twenty-three

I was pulled up into a funnel and stretched toward a small point of light, and into that point I flowed, as small as I'd ever been, as large as I'd ever been, everything and nothing at once, churning. There was light. Such light. A lot of light. All around. A brightness. And blinding heat. Searing fire that ebbed and washed. Cooling spaces. Circles that danced, orbs that moved. Smears of great numbers of these things all working in concert together, spirals of things that moved large exactly as they had moved small, for there was no scale here, just the same patterns, at every turn. There was a huge, enormous, massive, indisputable outward motion from every place and every thing, moving away from everything else, all of it going where it was supposed to be. I felt myself moving away from itself. Expanding. Stretching. Rising. Falling. Spreading. There was no up, no down, no forward, no back. Perfection. I was light. Then colors, and sounds, and harmonies, and music, and movement, and I was falling, falling, forever I fell, in every direction, at every speed, all at once.

And then I had feet, and there were drums.

I stood upon these feet, new feet, familiar and yet not, and they were whole, and bare, without pain, without scrapes or scratches. I was complete and I missed no one because everyone I knew and loved was also here, would also be here, had been here, came through here, was of this everythingness as well. I remembered all that came before and after. But I was exactly where I was supposed to be, and the music was so beautiful. My feet were made of music. I felt light as air upon them, and I was moved to dance.

And then there was space before me. Familiar space, not home, not the Vortex, but very like them both, yet different. The desert stretched out before me in every direction toward infinity. Six moons hung in the sky. And the sum total of it all moved. I moved, too. The music told us how, and where, and why, and what, and I was free.

And then there were people and animals. So many of them, some I had lost and known when I was someone else.

They moved with me, flowed along, and together we were perfect and I was new while being infinitely old. I sensed it was at the center out of which everything else spoked and spun. We had come from this place. We always came back to this place. I remembered it now and how it was in the past and would be in the future.

I felt joy, and I danced.

And the man came toward me, and the woman came toward me, and they were beautiful because we all were, and young, because we all were, and they held golden cups and they gave them to me and I drank. One was hot and one was cold. Both were right. I remembered this taste in my mouth, and I remembered their smiles, and I knew these people. They loved me, as I loved them, but there was no urgency in our reunion because we knew it was how it should be and would always be, back then and into forever, which flowed in all directions. There was laughter, and sound. We were so very old now, though we had only just been born. Their touch bore electricity, and I remembered this faintly from somewhere, this sensation, this fullness, this, ah—magic.

He touched me then, and she touched me then, and they pointed to a spot on the rock wall, where I was needed. I remembered this place from the future. There was a white light, and it moved with me, and I knew it as I knew that I must rise and join this beam of pure white light that came from the wall.

She told me to go in peace. He wished me happiness. They congratulated me on a life lived with love and compassion, music and beauty. She promised I'd see him again and I knew she told the truth. He would always wait for me, I would always wait for him.

I rose up, and the beam took me. It moved me toward the wall, and below they waved and the dance continued for the others, a constant stream of them breaking through, coming in, looking down to find feet they thought they'd lost, bodies whole and healthy, every need met, every question answered.

And I flew. Into the light. My grandmother. My great-grandfather. Others I had never met but instantly recognized. My future people from the past. Oddly, Gregory Hartwell was there, too, smiling at me like I was a long-lost daughter. I felt, overwhelmingly, that I was home. They reached for me as my feet came down. They touched me, welcomed me, loved me.

There was a gate that glowed and was made of pale blue light, a beautiful thing. Slowly it came open, and they welcomed me, and I wanted to be there. To stay. To rest. I raised a foot, and moved it forward, but it didn't go. It would not go. I cried out because there was a horrible pain I felt stabbing up through me in a place that was supposed to be free from pain. My neck. My neck. I held it and I screamed and boiling sounds came from my mouth, wet and dark, dark red. The people all looked at me in surprise. There was commotion.

Talking. Whispers and pointing. Gossip. Ripples came over the surface of what had been a smooth and infinite pond.

The voices said: *This has never happened before. This is something new. This is not right. This is not how it was written. This is not how the story is supposed to go.* They were afraid.

The light changed now, growing purplish, and the gate began to close and pulsate with an angry orange light. No longer welcome, and the patterns broke apart.

"No!"

I cried out for forward motion, but something pulled me backward, sucked me the wrong way. I grabbed for something, anything, to hold me in place, but there was only void. The voices were moving backward, too, a jumble of sound and time, and time was back again, where it had been gone before. The gate slammed shut. The arms reached for me. The smiles faded and in their place were screams of confusion, and cries of longing.

Sadness came to this place.

Reverse motion came for me, and pulled, and pulled, and pulled, until I was unstuck, and I went. Backward through a magnificent spiral, and kept moving, a nothing that sucked, pulled, forced, mashed me in a massive rotation, through the funnel, through a terrible screech, through a deafening sound that I knew, somewhere in the memory that came flooding back to me like blood from a wound, was the terrible, miraculous, impossible song of the Maker, resetting the gears of his clocks.

twenty-four

Rain fell onto my closed eyelids, and into my open mouth. I coughed down a gagging sensation, and gasped for air, my collapsed lungs filling again, hacking out whatever had drained into them. I rolled convulsively onto my side in the wet desert dust, and I heaved; I coughed up scabs and gooey blood clots from my throat into my mouth. The pain still gripped me, but it was fading, like the sound of a parade that has rounded the corner already. I remembered nothing for a moment, and wondered where I was. An angry sky, a barren landscape, sagebrush. Highway 550. The *descansos*. The word boomeranged back to me: Chaco. I'd been there.

I pushed myself to sitting, and wiped the rain and blood from my eyes, still coughing with the taste of iron and death in my mouth. I looked down and saw my feet, battered in torn black stockings. I wore a black party dress whose pretty pink sash was ripped and soiled, and lay in a miserable scribble on the ground at my side. I saw other feet then, two pairs. I looked up, stunned to remember I was not alone. Kelsey. My best friend. I remembered her now with a rush of love and happiness. She stared down at me with her jaw hanging slack and open, her blond hair flattened to the sides of her pretty face by the rain, her bright blue eyes blinking back tears, a strange sort of cry garbled in her throat, unable to come out, as if she were witnessing a birth, or a murder. Or both.

The brown cowboy boots belonged to Travis, a haunted look in his beautiful brown eyes.

"You did it." Kelsey finally managed to choke the words out in a hoarse whisper, shifting her eyes from me to Travis. "You did it. You brought her back to life."

Travis nodded solemnly, and looked to his right hand. Clutched in it was a bright, blindingly white stone that I recalled having seen somewhere before. On the ground at his feet lay a large, curved hunting knife, its half-serrated blade coated in blood and bits of flesh. My flesh.

I remembered now.

My hand rose to my neck, to the place where the knife had sunk in as easily as if it had been cutting cake. I touched it gingerly, lightly, just with my fingertips, not wishing to know what was there, but having to know at the same time. Astoundingly, there was only soft, smooth skin. No gaping incision, no bloody gash. Just me, as I had been before Victor killed me.

I turned my neck, and it moved smoothly; the bones no longer cracked and yanked back. My scalp no longer burned from the pulling of my hair. I was stunned, amazed, and, for a moment, ecstatic, until I remembered how sick and twisted Victor was, and realized that he could be anywhere. I spun around with a hunted look in my eyes, searching for him, and jumped up from sitting, landing in a defensive crouch.

"It's okay," Travis told me, his eyes wide with an unnamed worry, as though he was still processing what he'd done here. "He's gone. He got what he wanted."

I straightened to standing. Kelsey wept into her hands, and walked over to me, slowly, cautiously, muttering to herself that she could not believe what she had seen. Logan squirmed on the ground, still hog-tied, his eyes red with horror and flooded with tears of what seemed to be regret.

"The life stone," I said softly, touching Travis's hand that still held the stone.

"It was an emergency, right?" he said, taking my hands in his.

Overhead, the dark clouds gathered swiftly, churning above us as though a tornado might be forming. I had never seen the sky move like this in New Mexico, only in movies. It was agitated, and seemed alive. Travis eyed the storm warily, guiltily, sadly, and returned his gaze to me.

"I couldn't imagine never looking into your eyes again," he said. "I had to do it."

"But we would have found each other, right? I was in the Afterworld, Travis. You could have met me there, right?"

He shook his head. "I don't know for sure. Maybe. But I might not make it out of the Vortex. I couldn't risk losing you, or putting your friends and family through your loss. I—I don't know if I did the right thing, Shane. It just felt like I had to. I couldn't stand to see you like that."

"What happens now?" I asked, eyeing the sky.

"I don't know," he said plainly. I could tell that he was afraid, but resigned. "I'm just glad you're here."

"But what if you go now and I never see you?"

"I have faith the Maker rewards us for doing the right things, Shane. This was the right thing to do."

I collapsed into his arms. The familiar electricity was there, and flowed through me. I breathed deeply, relieved and still a bit disoriented.

Travis held me tightly, and I felt that his breathing was labored, wheezing, and his body felt weak. He wasn't the same Travis anymore. He seemed ill.

"Are you all right?" I asked, backing up to get a better

254

look at his face. He was terribly pale. Dark circles were starting to sink themselves around his eyes.

"It took so much out of him," said Kelsey. "Using that incredible energy to heal you."

Travis doubled over in pain, gripping his abdomen, groaning.

"Travis!" I cried, holding on to him as his body trembled and convulsed. "What's happening?"

He turned his eyes toward the sky, which churned as though it was opening a vortex of a new kind.

"They've come for me," he said, seeing something we could not. "I have to go."

"No!"

For a brief moment, his entire body flickered, like a flame that was about to go out, and for a split second, he disappeared. Then he was back, doubled over with pain once more, as though he'd been punched hard in the stomach.

"Travis!" I screamed. "No! What's going on?"

Struggling from the pain, he forced himself to stand against the increasingly violent wind. With a dignified expression, he looked me straight in the eye. He took both of my hands, and stepped toward me.

"I have to go now," he said.

"But where? The Vortex?"

His eyes were frightened as he shook his head no. He

wasn't going there, and this did not look like the beauty and peace of the Afterworld. He was going somewhere else.

"But why? You didn't do anything wrong!" I screamed.

"You shouldn't bring someone back from the dead," he said. "It messes with the order of things."

Travis locked eyes with me, resigned, stepped closer, and pulled me to him. "I have no regrets, Shane. I'm ready to face whatever it is. Maybe it was selfish, but I have faith that this way, I'll see you again."

Lightning flashed, and he flickered out, and reappeared, but paler than before, his breath even more ragged.

"No!" I shrieked, clinging to what was left of him. "Don't leave me! Don't leave me!"

In a raspy, weakening voice, he told me, "Find Randy. Tell him to watch over you until I figure out a way back. Victor's still out there. This is what he wanted"—Travis looked down at his flickering, fading body—"but it might not be enough. Tell Randy my wish is that he protect you."

"They can't do this to you!" I wailed.

Travis pulled as much strength into himself as he could, and lifted my chin with his hand, grimacing against whatever violence erupted and raged within him.

"I need to know if you're my Kindred," he said, looking

at my lips and then my eyes. "So do something for me."

"Anything!" I cried, desperate to keep him with me.

Travis smiled at me, beautiful as ever, and said, sorrowfully and simply, "Kiss me, Shane."

"But if we're not Kindreds . . . ," I whispered.

"Then I'll disappear immediately," he said. "But if we are, I'll have an extra minute. I have to know, Shane."

I nodded, and he stepped closer, embracing me in the growing tempest, as the wind whipped around us like witches laughing, and the stinging rain struck our faces like tiny bullets. He tilted his head to the side, and so did I, and I closed my eyes as our lips, at last, touched. A massive thunderclap marked the kiss, and I wasn't sure whether it was from this that I felt the earth move, or if it was from the kiss itself. He tasted like sunshine, like safety and beauty, and his lips sent a trembling, wonderful shock through me, to the center of my being, filled me with a deep, wonderful satisfaction and longing. I kissed him harder. There are no words to describe what that kiss felt like, only that it was, like everything else about Travis, perfectly suited to me. His kiss felt like home.

The wind kicked up more strongly, and began to wail. I heard Kelsey scream in fear, and I broke from the kiss to see what had startled her. Above us, the dark and menacing clouds sent down a funnel, shaped alternately like a finger or a tongue, pointed at the end and aimed directly at Travis. I was terrified it would take him immediately; but it seemed to pause in the air.

"It's halted!" he said, ecstatic, and then looked at me tenderly. "You are my Kindred."

I was overcome with a bittersweet happiness, followed by confused horror.

"Then you can't go! Right?"

He looked at the storm brewing and shook his head. He suddenly bent down, and grabbed my severed heart necklace from the ground.

"Touch this," he said, his speech difficult and labored. I did as he asked, and to my amazement, the pendant knit itself back together again, glowing with a shared energy from both of us. It was then that I spotted Victor, off to the side, watching the pendant with great interest. He wasn't gone. And whatever he saw in the necklace upset him a great deal, from the look on his face.

"He's still here," I told Travis.

Travis glanced at Victor just in time to see Victor disappear in a small tornado of his own conjuring, with a determined and unsavory smile upon his face. Travis turned his eyes back toward me.

"As my Kindred, you might be able to help me."

"How?" I cried. "What should I do?"

"Be open to me in dreams. I'll try to get back here. But if I can't, I know you can find me."

"Okay," I sobbed, as I nodded miserably.

The finger of blue-black cloud snaked down, closer and closer, and the wind wailed dreadfully, drawing him nearer to it.

"I love you," he called out, kissing me one last time, with great tenderness.

He stepped away from me now, doubled over in pain, as some unseen force seemed to beat him down, and he motioned with his hand for me to stand back, away from him. I collapsed onto my knees, devastated, and screamed with rage and misery into the assault from the sky. I wrapped my arms around myself, and I wept, and rocked like a madwoman. Kelsey ran to my side, knelt, and held me.

I watched in horror as the sky sent its dark tendril for Travis. Faces formed from the mist and shadows, devilish or human, tortured and imploring. Over the top of it all, laughter came, an evil laughter. I saw Victor's smiling face there among the others, sadistic and satisfied. Arms and hands and claws groped out from the tornado, seeking Travis. He watched the cloud descend upon him stonily; he must surely have been frightened, but he did not show it. Bravely he stood, tall and unflinching, and waited for the macabre funnel to find him.

He looked back at me one last time as he was pulled into its hideous midst. He lifted his chin, and with a courage I could not fathom, he tipped his hat as if everything were fine, to let me know I'd be okay. And then he was gone.

twenty-five

Two days passed without me sleeping, during which time we were all over the news.

Kelsey and I had been found on the side of Highway 550, near Travis's *descanso*, by passing motorists who'd seen us slouched there side by side, covered in blood. We'd lied a bit and said Logan alone had kidnapped us from the party, upset that I'd broken up with him, and that he'd tried to kill me. It was a lie of omission. We said nothing of Travis or Victor.

Police quickly found Logan's fingerprints on the knife, and arrested him at his parents' hunting cabin in Silver City later that first day. It was a huge scandal, given that he was the son of a state senator.

My mother wasn't letting me out of her sight. She

was convinced that I'd been battered and mentally harmed by my former boyfriend, and she now thought Logan was entirely to blame for my recent strange behavior. She was sure in her parental way that all of this was somehow her fault for having been a busy working mother and not a cuddly mommy who stayed home baking me cookies.

As for me? I was numb, distraught, like a soldier back from the battlefield, unbearably alone with my bottomless grief, with the shining exception of Kelsey, who believed me now, and kept my secrets with me.

It was the third day since Travis had gone, and there'd been no signs from him at all. I could not feel him anywhere. I was exhausted, on edge, hardly able to eat or drink, worn out. I lay on my bed feeling sick, my eyelids fluttering closed against my will. I did not want to sleep. What if he sent me a sign and I missed it? I felt like I was waiting up for someone to come home who never would again. I was afraid of sleep, afraid of the dark. Afraid of everything.

Nonetheless, sleep came for me in spite of my efforts to evade it. Sleep, like death, was inevitable, I thought as I slipped away. I tried to remain semiconscious as I drifted off, in case he came to me in dreams, but I did not dream, not that I could remember. Rather, I sank heavily into a placid liquid blackness, and there I rested, like a rock at the bottom of a well, until something eerie awakened me with a start.

I was stirred by the uncanny sense of a strange and foreign energy in the room with me, moving across me, over me, under me, and around the room like a slippery phantom, stopping here and there to watch me hungrily, as though rubbing its hands together in anticipation of my demise. I felt exposed, dirty, afraid, and violated. I tried to open my eyes to see who was there, but to my surprise I was unable to move at all, even to open my eyes. I was fully awake and aware, but I was completely paralyzed. Though I could not see who was in the room, I sensed its presence powerfully; I knew that it was a female, and she was very, very old—and very, very dangerous. I smelled her sulfuric odor of burned hair and rot, something about it reeking of underground, lava perhaps, mold, decay. The smell of death. I felt her cruelty in the way the air washed over me like a fetid whisper as she moved around, bringing a wake of terrible, intense cold with her.

I struggled against the paralysis, trying to get away. I wanted to sit up, to control my own body, but it was no use. Even my breathing was out of my control, too slow for my comfort; I felt like I was drowning in my own bed. I was stuck, my hands balled in fists, every muscle in my body tensed to the point of tortuous cramping, endless aching. If only I could open my hands, I thought strangely, then the dark stabbing energy that pinned me in place would flow out of me and I'd be released from this prison of immobilization. I tried, and tried, but could not relax my hands. Finally, though, I was able to open my eyes.

The room was dark, the house otherwise silent. Buddy did not stir, and I could not tell if this was because he did not sense the presence as I did, or because he, too, was paralyzed by it. Then I saw it: an even deeper, eternal sort of darkness superimposed itself across the gloom; it was alive, a spindly black demonic force hovering in the air between me and the ceiling, with legs and arms that moved slowly and deliberately, like an insect-person swimming leisurely underwater. She had a hunched back, and long white hair tied up with some sort of scarf, and hands with long, sharp fingernails. I wanted to scream, but nothing came out. I could not control anything now but my eyes, and I did not like what I saw.

"Shane," the thing whispered evilly, in a strange, wispy croak that seemed to come from very far away. "Shane . . ."

My heart began to race, but my breath did not match its pace. Again I began to feel that I might drown in the air. I wasn't getting enough oxygen. I'd suffocate soon. But how did it know my name? What was it? Why was it here?

The thing—and I cannot call it a woman, exactly,

because it had a tail and claws—opened its mouth to reveal sharp yellow teeth and fangs. Her nose was pressed up and into her face like a bat's. Her tongue darted out, thin like a snake's, and tested the air between us.

"Shane," she whispered again, drifting closer to me, undulating.

I prayed. There was no other power I had now but the power of my own thoughts. I ran through the words in my mind, again and again, praying for her to be gone, for me to be free of the grip she had over me. Nearer yet she drifted, until her hideous, wrinkled, sunken old bat face with her eerily glowing yellow eyes and enormous pointed ears was only inches from my own.

"So this is the Shane he thinks of so often," she hissed.

Suddenly, she moved fast in a burst of energy, curling into a hunched ball and squatting hard upon my chest. I could not breathe as her weight crushed me. The contact with her filled my body with a cold, slushy sensation. I felt her spindly, frozen hands clamp with astonishing strength upon my neck and begin to squeeze fervently.

"He will never escape," she cackled hysterically. "You will not take him from me, Shane. You will not live to find him. Oh, how long I've waited for something so good, so sweet, so delicious as he! He's mine now. All mine . . ."

My mind raced in a panic, and I knew that the only hope I held was in the power of my own thoughts. I remembered the look of calm and faith Travis had as the sky pulled him in, and I tried to find that same attitude for myself now. *You will not take me,* I said in my mind, *you cannot take me. I have faith and you will never defeat me.* I visualized all that was good, and I filled my heart with love. *You cannot take this from me. You can never destroy true love or faith. I will find him. You cannot stop me. He is my Kindred, and there is no one and nothing that will keep me from him.*

I focused these thoughts as tightly as a laser's point, and aimed them at her, from my mind, and I told her she would let go of me. *You cannot hold me, you cannot touch me, you will not touch me, you will leave this place and go back to where you came from, and you will not come back.*

She cackled.

"You pitiful, stupid girl," she hissed, her voice sounding like many voices at once. But her hands released my throat, and her crushing weight began to lighten upon me. It was working! Whatever I was doing, it was working!

I focused on more beautiful thoughts and visualized surrounding myself with a pure white bubble of peace and happiness that she could not penetrate, and I imagined light filling it with good energy. *You're not welcome here,* I willed.

She screamed now, her laugh turning to a bloodcurdling

cry of frustration. I watched as she backed up and off of me, floating up toward the ceiling as her face twisted in fury.

"Where is the pendant?" she demanded.

Love will always conquer hate, I said in my mind, and chanted it over and over. She began to twist in agony, writhing angrily as she lost control of me. I focused now on my hands, feeling that if I could open them, it would help force her away.

"Don't you want to know where he is?" she screamed, sensing my increasing strength. "Don't you want me to lead you to him? I can do that! I can take you to him right now if you want! Just tell me where the pendant is. You should hear how he cries for you, like a little baby. You're the only one who can save him, you know. His Kindred."

I hesitated and wavered in my focus. But my heart came back strong and told me that she was lying, trying to trick me into submission once more so that she could finish me off. This horrible creature, whatever she was, wanted Travis all to herself.

Love will always conquer hate. He loves me and I love him and you are not welcome here. This is a loving home, and I am a loving girl. You are not to be here.

I zeroed in on my hands, and willed them to open. I knew from Travis that energy travels through your hands, and I realized that unless I could open my fists, the dark force would remain inside of me. With all my might, I willed them to open. And finally, mercifully, they did.

As soon as my fists relaxed, the demonic presence in my room disappeared, her evil energy flowing right out of my hands like water, and cascading through the floor, back to whatever sickening place it had come from.

Instantly, I could breathe again.

I was covered in sweat, my heart racing, and my chest felt bruised where she had crushed me. I sat up, and my neck hurt terribly. Buddy began to bark ferociously now, hysterical, growling at the very corner where I had seen the apparition—or demon, or whatever it was—sink away into the dead of night.

Chilled and terrified, I began to sob uncontrollably. What had it been? What was it trying to do? Were things only going to get worse for me now that Travis was gone? Who was going to save me now?

My mother came running into the room to see what the commotion was.

"It sat on my chest," I told her, trembling as she turned on the light.

"What did you say?" she asked, and for the first time I could remember during this entire ordeal since my car accident, my mother's expression changed from one of judgmental doubt and worry to one of pure, unbridled horror.

"Shane," she said softly, sitting next to me on the bed with her eyes zeroing in on my neck. "What happened to you, honey?"

"What do you mean?" I asked.

She pointed. "There are marks all over your neck," she said, fear in her eyes.

I bolted out of bed and ran to look in the mirror. I saw two large handprints, one on each side of my throat, where the creature had tried to strangle me. The finger marks were thin and long, not human, and in places the skin was raised and bleeding where she'd scraped me with her claws.

"Who did this to you?" my mother asked, coming to stand behind me. "Logan? Was he here? Did you see him again?"

"No, not Logan. It was a monster."

I told my mother everything about what had happened, but instead of her finally believing me, she began to cry.

"I don't like what's happening to you," she said. The way she said it startled me.

"You think I do?"

"Shane, could you be doing this to yourself?" she asked. "I think that all of this could be some kind of a cry for help."

"Didn't you hear the monster?" I asked her. "It was hissing at me, talking to me. It was right here, Mom! I wouldn't make something like that up! I can't!"

"Shane, I don't want you to take this the wrong way, honey, but we might want to think about sending you to a specialist. I know a good place up north, for young adults who have been through a great deal of trauma."

"What?" I asked. "You mean a mental hospital?"

"It's an in-treatment center," she corrected me, but the distinction was meaningless. My mother was talking about having me locked up. She was starting to cry. "Mental illness is nothing to be ashamed of, okay? We'll get you the help you deserve."

I was devastated by her words, and too weak after what had happened to me to argue. Slowly, I shuffled back to my bed, and crawled beneath my covers. She'd never believe me. There was nothing I could do.

"Leave me alone, then," I said. I didn't like the way she was looking at me anymore, or what she was saying about me. "Get out."

"I'm just trying to help you, Shane. I love you. I'd do anything to help you, honey."

"Get out!" I screamed, throwing a pillow at her. "Now! Get out of here!"

"I'm making you an appointment with a psychiatrist," she said, inching toward the door to leave. "We're going to get to the bottom of this. We'll figure out the best next steps. We're going to get you better, honey."

I left the lights on and did not sleep again that night, dreading the thing's return.

Only two thoughts gave me hope as I waited for the sun to rise and a new day to begin.

One, that the disgusting clawed thing, whatever it was, had talked about Travis as though he was still present somewhere, and she'd said he thought of me. She had also said that only I had the power to save him, which meant that it wasn't too late for him to be saved. I didn't know if that was true, but I chose to believe it anyway.

Two, Kelsey was still my best friend, and she believed me now. I thought of calling her, but I didn't want to wake her. When morning finally came, I would call, and tell her everything, and I wouldn't be alone with the insanity that had become my life. I got up and quietly began to pack a small suitcase with my belongings; when dawn broke, I planned to go to my best friend's house and try to fix my life from there. I couldn't stay in my mother's house anymore. I needed support.

twenty-six

L ater that day, Kelsey went with me to the university physics department, and stood at my side as I knocked on the door of Mr. Hedges's office. He answered, and looked surprised to find us there. He invited us into an office that was as messy and chaotic as he was. He cleared a couple of chairs opposite his desk of junk food wrappers and random wads of paper, and we sat. No longer worried about sounding crazy, I explained it all to him, from the crash to now. To my surprise, Mr. Hedges listened without seeming to find me nuts. In fact, he leaned forward farther and farther the more I talked, his face twitching with fascination and excitement.

"This happened out near Chaco Canyon, you say?" he asked when I had finished.

"Yes, sir."

Mr. Hedges rubbed his hands together happily. "Oh, yes! I'm not surprised. I chose this university because of its proximity to that very place. You girls do know that Chaco is one of the hot spots around the world for ley lines?"

"What's a ley line?" I asked.

"They are earth-energy lines," he answered. "Some people call them spirit lines. I have been hoping to find a portal, and it sounds from what you've said that you found one."

"I think so."

"This is wonderful!" he exclaimed.

"Yeah," said Kelsey cynically. "All except for the parts where I had to watch a demon try to murder Shane, and, you know, where the love of her life was scooped up by a tornado from hell."

Mr. Hedges frowned. "As a physicist, I'd really prefer you didn't use strictly religious terms for these things."

"Whatever you want to call it," said Kelsey. "Can you help us find Travis or not?"

"Terribly exciting," he mumbled to himself, and began stirring the mess of papers on his desk. "Very, very, oh yes."

"Have you actually traveled to any of these dimensions?" I asked him.

Mr. Hedges shook his head. "Not exactly, no. But I am close to perfecting the calculations to do so."

"Great," said Kelsey unhappily. She looked at me as though we were wasting our time.

Mr. Hedges found a business card among the mess of papers, and handed it over to me. Lowering his voice to a whisper, he said, "I shouldn't probably tell you girls this, because it makes me sound like a total crackpot, but there is a medium I work with who is able to see into the dimensions. She has guides there. She has been incredibly helpful to me, but I cannot, of course, tell anyone here about her. You understand."

"Yes," I said, looking at the card for Minerva Montoya, psychic. "I know what it's like to have people think you're crazy. My own mom is talking about having me institutionalized because of all of this."

"Then we are of a like mind, you and I," said Mr. Hedges, still whispering. "I suggest you ask her what to do next, and then we'll talk again. I'm sorry I couldn't be of more help, but the spiritual and emotional part of this does not interest me as much as the mathematics of it."

"I understand," I told him, feeling hopeless.

"Off you go, then," said Mr. Hedges, standing and opening the door. His social skills were just as awkward here as they were at our school.

Half an hour later, Kelsey and I sat in a café in the Nob

Hill district of the city, nursing lattes and trying to make sense of things. I did not like the turn my life had taken. I needed resolution, and peace. I could not go on living like this. I *would* end up in a mental hospital.

The café sat directly across the street from the purple door that led to the office of Minerva Montoya, psychic medium. We could see the office and its sign through the window next to our booth. So far, no one had come or gone from it.

"She spelled *your* wrong," said Kelsey, jutting her chin toward the purple door.

I looked at the hand-painted sign. Sure enough, it read FOR ALL YOU'RE SPIRITUAL NEEDS.

"But maybe spelling isn't a requirement for being a psychic. We should really pay the lady a visit, and just see what she says."

Minutes later, we sat across from Minerva Montoya herself, in her Nob Hill office, which was really just the living room of her small and disorganized apartment above the shoe store. Stacks of newspapers formed walls within the walls of the place, and we'd had to navigate a maze just to get to the red loveseat upon which we sat, side by side, trying to ignore the fact that a crust of old bread had sprung out from the cushions behind us. A massive cockroach crawled quite slowly up the nearest wall, and the place smelled of many cats and overripe fruit. If this were a month ago, I would have run from the apartment convinced on appearances alone that Minerva Montoya was an unsanitary crackpot; but I was now the girl who'd been brought back from the dead by a ghost. I didn't have much room to judge anybody anymore.

Minerva was a pudgy middle-aged woman with wild, wavy dark hair streaked with gray that frizzed out of the bottom of her large pink hat. She sat in a low wingback chair, and when she crossed her legs underneath her gauzy, flowing skirt, she exposed her rainbow-striped leg warmers and Birkenstock sandals. On top she had a thick woolen sweater and a shawl. It all looked hastily handmade and odd, but despite that, Minerva still managed to be quite alluring somehow, and I felt comforted and soothed by the patient, knowing expression in her eyes.

"I've been expecting you," she said, leaning forward to pour tea for us. The cups were not exactly clean, and so I took just the tiniest sip, as politeness dictated I must.

"You have?" I asked, still skeptical. "Did Mr. Hedges call?"

Minerva look confused, and shook her head. "Clyde? No. Why? Should he have?"

"I don't know. He's our teacher. He told us to see you."

She laughed. "Oh. No. That's not it. I knew yesterday you'd be here. What I mean to say is, I didn't know *exactly* who would be arriving, but I knew there were two girls coming into my life who needed guidance about a spiritual matter. And here you are."

I felt goose bumps rise on my arms, because I knew she was genuine. In the past, I would have doubted all of what she said, but now I knew better. Minerva looked at us both for a long time without speaking. Kelsey and I had agreed to tell her nothing, in order to see if she could figure out what we wanted. Soon, the psychic's eyes came to rest only on me.

"It's you," she said. "Your friend here loves you very much, and you are fortunate to have her with you during this difficult time."

I felt that now-familiar chill that comes when you witness something unusual. Kelsey and I remained stock-still, and offered no more information.

"You're testing me," said Minerva with a sly smile as she sipped some tea. "That's fine. I understand. When you've been through as much as you have, it's hard to know who to trust, isn't it?"

Kelsey and I exchanged a significant look, but still said nothing.

Minerva closed her eyes for a moment, then opened them to stare at me once more.

"I feel a darkness upon you," she told me. "You are marked. Something has come from the Underworld and touched you. It has left its scent."

Goose bumps rose across my arms, and the hair on the back of my neck stood on end.

"Some houses or buildings are haunted," she continued. "And sometimes people are haunted. You are haunted by this dark entity now. Shadowed by it. It is not a ghost. It is not human. It is here with us now, lurking, trying to get in. I won't let her. She is not allowed here."

I gasped. Minerva reached out to me and took my hand.

"Don't be frightened. She feeds off of that. You have fought her off already, or you would not be here. You know instinctively that she is afraid of goodness and love. These are the best weapons you have against her."

"Who is she?" I asked, my voice faint with fear.

"She is known by many names. Maera, Mara, Bakhtak. Most often, she is called the Old Hag in the English tradition. She is a very old, very hateful female demon who comes when you are sleeping and sits upon your chest to suffocate you."

Kelsey and I both widened our eyes in amazement.

"Am I correct?" asked Minerva.

"Yes," I said. "She came to me for the first time last night."

"I can talk to her," said Minerva, "but it is very draining, and very dangerous for me and for my spirit guides. I'm keeping her at bay right now with their help. She is furious with you for some reason. A necklace, I think." Her brow furrowed with deep concern. "Do you have any idea what that might be?"

I nodded, and was about to tell Minerva about Travis when Kelsey interrupted me.

"Minerva, shouldn't you be able to know why?" Kelsey asked her.

Minerva turned her eyes toward my best friend and smiled in patient offense. "Still testing me, I see."

"We just have to be sure," said Kelsey. "I'm sorry if that offends you. There is a lot for us to lose here."

"Then give me a moment," said Minerva, a hint of frustration in her voice. "I'm listening to her now. She is not someone I wish to invite into my space, but your friend here needs my help very much. Her life is in danger. Be quiet so I can hear the Old Hag, please."

Minerva's eyes rolled back in her head, and she began to whine and rock. I felt a sudden wave of anxiety as the presence of the Old Hag returned to me.

Finally, Minerva's eyes popped open, and she smiled at us as though seeing us for the first time in a very long while.

"Well, hello, girls," she said.

Kelsey looked at me, and I shrugged almost imperceptibly.

"You are so, so special, Shane," Minerva said warmly,

tears flowing freely from her eyes as she got up to come and squeeze herself onto the sofa next to me now. She held me tightly to her bosom and released me with a heavy sigh. I had not told her my name, and Kelsey knew it. If there was any doubt that this woman was the real deal, it was gone.

"You have found your soul mate," she said to me joyfully, "but he is on the other side, is this right?"

I began to cry, and in a flood of words, I told her everything, from the moment of the crash up until an hour before in the café. Minerva listened attentively until I was through.

"So what do you hope to get from me?" she asked. "How can I be of use to you?"

"I want to know what to do now," I told her. "Travis said I could help him, he asked me to find him. I don't know how to do that. I want to know if we can figure out where he is, and how to get him back from there. He saved me, and it's my turn to save him. I know it."

"I see," she said thoughtfully. "This is a new one for me. I've been doing this for many years, but I've never run into a situation like this. Let me see if I can find him, dear."

Tense with excitement and fear, I waited as the medium closed her eyes again. Kelsey and I looked at each other, and I could tell that she shared my nervousness and that she believed Minerva. The medium began to mumble and murmur, rocking so violently at one point that Kelsey and I both had to lean far from her to avoid being smashed into.

After about ten minutes of this, Minerva's eyes snapped open again, and again she said, "Well, hello, girls," as though she had forgotten where she was or who we were for a moment. She composed herself then, coughed for a full minute, and finally spoke.

"He exists," she said. "This much I know. I feel echoes of him in various corners of the cosmos. He's not gone. The Old Hag speaks of him, and for this reason I believe he is with her, or near her, but I am sorry to say I cannot contact him directly at this time."

"Why not?" I cried.

"I need something of his," she said apologetically. "The Old Hag is standing in my way, and won't let me through. If I could physically touch something that he'd once held in his hand, that he loved, then I could find him more easily."

"What about me?" I asked. "He's touched me. He loves me."

Minerva's eyes softened as though she found my naïveté adorable. "No, dear, that doesn't work. Your own spirit would overpower whatever other spirits are on your flesh. I need an inanimate object. A hairbrush, or something he wore, a shirt. Jewelry works especially well. Metal is always good."

"We'll find something," Kelsey blurted.

"We don't have anything like that," I reminded Kelsey.

"I know. But we could," she said.

Minerva continued, "I just need to be able to pull some of his energy and his vibration into myself so that when I seek him on the other side I will be able to find him more easily."

"Where are you looking for him?" I asked. "In the Vortex?"

"No. In the Underworld," she said. "That is where I feel he is most likely to be found now."

"Is he stuck there?" I asked.

Minerva shrugged and sighed. "I don't know. Probably, because I cannot find him by calling for him. I have a very good network of guides who are able to find almost anyone I seek on the other side. But if you're his soul mate, then what the Old Hag says makes sense. You can probably enter the Underworld and bring him back, but only you can do that. This is probably why she fears and hates you so much. She loves having him there. I think she feeds off of darkening his positive energy. When he is scared or lonely or sad, when he feels hopeless, she thrives."

"How will I be able to reach him?" I asked, horrified by the idea of going to the Very Bad Place. "Would I have to die again?"

She smiled at me. "No, dear. Of course not. I would never assist you if that were the case."

"Then how?"

"There are other ways. Clyde is working on travel to other dimensions. Did he tell you this?"

Kelsey and I nodded.

Minerva continued. "Yes, he's quite close. We just needed to nail down an actual portal location, but it sounds as though you might know where that is?"

"Yes," I said.

"Good. Then we are in good shape, relatively. But first we have to figure out where Travis is. Do you have something of his I can use to pick up on his energy? If we were to just randomly enter the Underworld, we might never find him."

"But I don't have anything of his," I said desperately.

"I know where we can find something, though," said Kelsey.

"What?" I asked, shocked.

"You should do this soon," said Minerva sagely. "The Old Hag is dangerous and very real. There are many people throughout all of history who are said to have quietly died in their sleep. People say their hearts just stopped, or something of that nature. That is usually not what happened. In such cases, the Old Hag has taken them. She feeds on the energy of human souls. She needs a lot of them. She is voracious and said to want to rule the known universe."

"You think she'll kill Shane?" asked Kelsey.

Minerva took one of my hands, and one of Kelsey's, and said, "Not if we can help it, she won't. Now, go. Get that something of Travis's and bring it back to me right away."

Kelsey was already up, preparing to go, but I had one last question for Minerva.

"If we do this, and I get him back, is there any way my life will ever go back to normal again?" I asked. "I can't imagine living around people like my mom who don't believe me, hiding the truth for the rest of my life."

Minerva's eyes grew sorrowful, and I knew she understood personally what I was saying.

"I am sorry to say your life will never be the same," she told me as she looked about her, as though remembering something from her own life. "But I am happy to tell you that you will become strong and smart enough through this journey to be able to navigate the rapids of humanity in a way that keeps you safe from their misunderstandings. You will have a happy life, Shane, if you do this right. And whomever you lose to them thinking you are crazy, you will find new friends who understand you."

We left then. Kelsey hurried out to the street, and practically ran to her hybrid car.

"Here," she said, tossing me the keys. "You drive."

"Me? Why?"

"Because I'm the navigator," she said, whipping her smartphone out of her handbag.

"Where are we going?" I asked.

"You're driving us down to Belen," she said with a conspiratorial grin on her face. "There's this widow who runs a ranch out there. I think we need to use her bathroom because we got lost trying to find a dog breeder and, like stupid city girls, we can't bring ourselves to squat behind a tree."

"What?" I asked, completely confused.

"Just drive," she said.

twenty-seven

Kelsey and I drove along Highway 47, south through the Isleta Indian reservation with its massive Hard Rock Hotel and Casino, through the suburb of Los Lunas, past farms, trailers, and long-abandoned adobe dwellings, following the scribble of water that was this area's only major river. The ranch was set back from the highway a mile or so on a dirt lane, accessed by passing beneath a large metal arch bearing the name Hartwell Ranch.

The ranch appeared to be about forty acres, with stables and corrals. The horses wore blankets over their backs and seemed strong and well cared for. I spied the pinkish-beige stucco pitched-roof house set back from the farmland, with its large wraparound porch and three-car garage. A big, healthy family house. I wasn't sure why this surprised me, or why I had assumed Travis would have been raised in a small, dumpy house or trailer. I guess it was because he was from Valencia County, his speech had a twang, and he wore a cowboy hat. I was embarrassed by how little I knew about the lives people lived in the rural countryside so close to my own home.

As we drove over the bumpy road, alongside a fallow, frozen field, toward the house, two large dogs gave chase on the field side of the fence, yapping and barking. I had the strangest feelings coursing through me as I looked at the place. This was my one true love's home. It felt familiar to me somehow, as though he'd imparted a sense of the place to me through his touch. I felt I'd been here before, though I knew that was utterly impossible. It felt haunted by him, by Randy, too, just a little, and I tried to picture them as children here, playing, working, growing up. A shroud of sadness hung over the ranch, too, and it was palpably a place of undeserved sorrow. A place wrapped in a veil of shouldn't-have-beens. A place of ghosts.

I parked in the driveway, and cut the engine. It was so quiet, and I felt so odd, as though I might see Travis come bursting out of the front door. I wondered what that might have been like, the two of us dating like normal teenagers, if he'd lived. But I probably never would have met him, he said so himself. The question was moot. It would never be.

Kelsey and I quickly went over our plan, agreed upon it, and exited the car. We walked to the door, and rang the buzzer. We were waiting for someone to answer from inside the house, but as it happened, our answer came from outside, from behind us.

"Can I help you?" called a tough woman's voice.

I spun to see a trim, seemingly strong woman who was probably in her late forties or early fifties, standing maybe fifteen feet from us, holding a wooden-handled ax. She wore jeans, work boots, and a large flannel jacket that seemed like it might once have belonged to a man because of the way she had the sleeves rolled into thick cuffs. Her hair was back in a ponytail, and she had a kerchief tied around her head the way some women did when they performed chores. Her face was pretty for her age, though she did not seem to wear makeup or carry herself in a way that said prettiness mattered to her, and in her expression and the set of her jaw I instantly saw Travis. He had her soulful brown eyes, and her dark hair and full mouth. They were so alike that I gasped a little at the sight of her, and had to work very hard to retain my composure in order to effectively pull off our plan. There was no doubt about it. This was my Kindred's mother.

"Hi!" Kelsey called out cheerily, always having been a

better actress than I was.

"Hello," the woman replied politely but coolly. She didn't smile. I wondered if she ever did anymore. I could not imagine the pain she had suffered in her life, losing everyone she loved, having herself perhaps been brutalized by Victor. He'd taken everything from her, and I loathed him.

"We're sorry to bother you, ma'am," Kelsey continued, even though in the plan it was supposed to be me doing most of the talking. She probably knew I was frozen with shock. "We were just down here looking to get a puppy from a breeder, but the address we had was wrong, and we got lost, and now, and this is the embarrassing part, we really have to pee."

The woman cracked a bitter half grin that seemed a good bit annoyed, though I couldn't tell what annoyed her more: the fact that we were the type to buy designer dogs, or the fact that we didn't know how to pee in the countryside. She sneaked a look at Kelsey's shiny hybrid Prius, and smirked to herself. It was not the sort of car you found on ranches, generally.

"Come on in," she said. "Let me just put this ax out back. Be right there."

Kelsey and I exchanged a significant look that marked our success with step one of our mission. The woman returned with a stern, carefully guarded expression on her face, and opened the door with a set of keys. I noticed she unlocked three locks on it, even though this was the sort of area where most people felt safe leaving doors unlocked. If I had been her, I would have done the same thing. She knew the tragedy life could dish out unexpectedly. She wanted no more loss. She was never going to be vulnerable again.

The house was spotless, and spacious, decorated in a no-nonsense middle-class style that reminded me of the rooms you'd see in department store catalogs. The floors were of tile in places and pristine cream-colored carpet in others. The furniture was high-quality, but not showy, wholly functional, which spoke of a certain kind of family that might sit down to homemade chicken potpie. We'd never had anything like that; my mother had always preferred to microwave ready-made food for me, or to get takeout from the gourmet market's deli, because she was so busy. Travis's mom seemed busy, too, running a horse ranch; but she seemed like the type who'd make time for family and cooking. It smelled of potpourri in the house, apples and cinnamon, and of a pot roast cooking. Photos were in a variety of charmingly mismatched frames everywhere you looked, so many photos: photos of Travis and Randy, Randy and Travis, as babies, toddlers, children, teens.

This house was no longer a home; it was a shrine.

"There's one off the kitchen there, and another down

the hall past the door, there," said Travis's mother, looking at us curiously as we made much of squirming to hold our bladders in control. Kelsey went for the kitchen, leaving me to the hallway.

I hurried down the somewhat darkened corridor, noticing the walls were coated with photos, many from rodeo contests, all of them bearing Travis's face. The locket around my neck warmed and glowed more and more brightly as I took in these pictures, and I covered it with my hand to stifle the light. My heart ached terribly, and I fought back tears. I missed him with such fervor it threatened to topple me. He'd been so talented, so decorated, and he'd had such a lovely mother. Such a pleasant home. Such potential for joy and greatness, and the family through no fault of its own had been caught in Victor's crosshairs. It wasn't fair. None of it was fair. Where I had simply felt a fear and resentment of Victor, within the walls of this house I now felt a vengeful streak rise like anger in me. I wanted to take him down for what he'd done to this family, to my love, and to me.

I found the bathroom, stepped in, and closed the door. It was a green-and-white wonderland of shine and gleam, spacious and filled with living plants in pots with crocheted holders, more photos, and perfect towels and little dishes of soaps in the shape of seashells. Like the rest of the house, it smelled freshly scrubbed and as though no one had ever done in it what bathrooms were known for. It was pleasant, but also almost unfathomably sad, because the woman who tended to it all had clearly not moved on, was not ever going to move on. She was keeping things as they had been, in perfect working order for the day when those who'd once shared this space with her would return.

I knew how she felt, and yet I dreaded becoming like her. How could I not? Travis's pull was so strong, and our love for each other so perfect and enormous, there would be no moving on from him. There simply couldn't be. I had to find him. I had to save him. I had to bring him back into my world, because a life without Travis was unthinkable now. And this, I reminded myself, was why I was here, in this house, now. To steal a piece of him from her. I didn't want to add to her misery, or take anything away, but I reasoned that in doing so I could possibly bring back part of him to her world.

Because I didn't actually need to go to the bathroom, I waited a moment, then washed my hands, drying them on one of the stiff green towels that smelled of dryer sheets and felt like it was never used.

I cracked the door open, and listened. Kelsey, true to our plan, was busily asking Travis's mom a million questions, trying to get her to let Kelsey see her horses. While she carried on in this way, I sneaked down the hall another couple of doors, until I came to the room I felt belonged to

Travis. I did not feel his hand or thoughts guiding me as I had in dreams, but I just knew. I entered and recognized the room as surely as if it had been my own, and wondered if somehow Travis had transferred knowledge to me in my sleep.

I went directly to the wooden shelf affixed to the wall above the dresser. It veritably sagged with fancy trophy belt buckles, dozens and dozens of them, all with his name on them and many demonstrating he'd won first place. I ran my fingers over them, my lip caught between my teeth and my brow furrowed with concentration, trying to remember which was the one he had loved the most. His soul was my soul, I told myself. Even if I could no longer feel *him*, I could feel what he'd felt, if I just allowed it to happen. I stopped on a small buckle, worn down and nondescript. He'd been four years old when he won it, according to the date. It was for something called "mutton busting" and he'd come in first place. It was the oldest trophy here, and from the warmth I felt emanating from it, his most precious. His first win, the time when he first realized he had a calling for rodeo. I swiped the little buckle, stuffed it easily into the pocket of my jacket. I hustled out of the room as quickly as I could, ducked down the hall, and found Kelsey standing with Travis's mom at the far end of the kitchen, pointing at something outside. Seeing me, she stopped.

"Hi," I said as naturally as I could fake.

"All set?" Travis's mom asked me. I could tell Kelsey was getting on her nerves.

"Yes, thank you so very much." I shot Kelsey a knowing look so she'd understand I'd accomplished our mission.

"You're a lifesaver," Kelsey said to Travis's mom. I didn't know if my friend recognized the irony in her choice of words, but I certainly did.

"You girls need directions out of here?" Travis's mother asked, almost seeming sad to see us go. I wondered if she ever had guests or visitors.

"Sure," Kelsey said, though we didn't. As Mrs. Hartwell told us how to get back to the interstate, I felt an overwhelming urge to throw my arms around her, to tell her how sorry I was, to ask her if I could come and visit her often. I wanted to tell her I'd seen him, I knew him, that both her sons were still out there somewhere. But I couldn't do any of that. I couldn't risk having her think me crazy, too. I didn't want to open up old wounds for her, or clog her life with any more turmoil or pain.

"Thank you, Deidre," I said, as she showed us to the door. "Have a wonderful day."

She looked at me in surprise.

"How did you know my name?" she asked me.

Caught, I waffled and blushed. I stammered and tried to think up a lie. "Um, I, uh, I saw it on the mailbox,

Hartwell Ranch, and then in the hall, the pictures, there was something with your name."

In truth, I knew her name from the news stories I'd read about the deaths of her sons. She narrowed her eyes at me, sensing the lie, her body growing rigid with defensiveness as she seemed to wonder who might have sent us here. Where she'd previously seemed only sad, she now seemed afraid. I wanted so much to tell her she did not need to fear us, but I couldn't.

"Kids around here generally refer to adults as Mister and Missus," she said suspiciously, "in case you girls ever get 'lost' again."

"Thanks," Kelsey said, shoving me out the door. "Have a great day!"

Travis's mother gave us a mournful look and did not answer. Her eyes were wide with worry now, but also filled with painful memories she had no idea I understood as deeply as I understood my own being. The ache I held in the center of my heart for Travis expanded in that moment to include his mother, and I felt dizzy with grief—but with the trophy in hand, and Minerva maybe able to help me find him, I was hopeful for the first time. As we walked out of the house, the heat from my locket grew stronger, and I pulled it out from under my shirt to keep it from scorching my skin.

twenty-eight

Going as fast as we legally could, Kelsey and I returned to Minerva's oddball apartment in the city, with Travis's childhood trophy like a prize in my hand. Minerva was knitting something shapeless and fuzzy, and she welcomed us as though we were old friends back from a yearlong journey. We quickly got down to the business of her trying to find traces of Travis's spiritual energy on the award.

Kelsey and I once again sat on the red sofa with the bread crust in it, and we watched as Minerva, seated in the wingback chair, closed her eyes and turned the belt buckle over and over in her hands, mumbling, "Yes . . . yes . . . oh yes . . . I see. . . ." She touched every part of it, caressed it, and little by little a satisfied smile crept onto her face. It put me at ease, that smile, because it was truly and genuinely happy, and I waited to hear what she'd say next. My heart raced, and I was filled with hope. I'd find him. I knew I would.

"He was so happy when he got this," said Minerva, opening her eyes and raising her gaze to the ceiling. "I can see a little boy, such a cute little thing, just beaming, his whole face a smile. I sense his father, too. A proud father. They were very close, even though the boy never knew his dad was with him; his dad was there when he won this. At all his wins, I think."

Minerva's eyes shifted back down and connected with mine.

"His father is here, with us," she told me.

"What?" I asked, incredulous.

"He wasn't here before," mused Minerva, "so I am thinking he must be connected to this buckle as well. You brought him with you. You have alerted him to your presence."

"Is he mad at us?" I asked.

"Not at all," said Minerva. "But he does have an anger he has carried for a very long time, long before he became aware of us here in this room. He is not a peaceful spirit. He feels guilty, as though somehow he could have saved his family. But it isn't his fault, and we need to help him to understand this so that he can move on to where he needs to go."

She focused on a spot across the room, and said, "Gregory, welcome. We are all friends here, and we all want what is best for your son Travis. Please feel at home with us. We mean you and your family no harm."

Again, my skin crawled with goose bumps, and I shivered. Kelsey crossed her arms over her chest and pulled her knees together protectively.

Minerva began to meditate upon the buckle again, and again fell into a trancelike state as, I assumed, she searched for Travis. Five minutes later or so, her eyes popped open and her gaze bore into me. She rose and came to sit at my side again, holding the buckle in one hand and my hand in her other.

"I've got the energy," she said, "but it took a moment to register because his energy is so much like yours. Let me compare."

She lowered her head in concentration, and a few held breaths later, looked up brightly.

"Oooh," she said, as if in awe.

"What?" I asked.

"You're a musician, right?" she asked me. I nodded, and she kept talking. "Then you understand that musical notes are just vibrations that your eardrum picks up."

"Of course."

"That's kind of what spirits are like for me," she said.

"Think of me as a person who was born with a kind of ear, here"—she touched her sternum—"that allows me to hear spiritual vibrations. They really are very much like music."

"Okay."

"There are tones, and frequencies, and harmonies," she explained, still smiling at me in a sort of joyful awe, "and each spirit has a slightly different sort of harmony to it. Kindred spirits vibrate together in complete and perfect unison. This is very rare, indeed, and each person is only given one—one!—Kindred, or perfect soul mate, and oftentimes, they never meet."

I waited, my heart pounding. I knew what would come next—the pause in the tornado had told us—but I needed to hear it out loud, as a fact.

"Shane, you and Travis sound in perfect unison. It is no wonder, then, that when you and Travis touched there was a special and compelling energy. You were part of the same soul finding itself again, making itself whole."

"Oh my God," I said.

"No wonder his absence is incredibly painful."

"That is so amazing," said Kelsey.

"Do you know where he is?" I asked Minerva.

"I get a feeling about it," she told me, "but given that you are a Kindred, I would bet that a part of you knows where he is."

"I wish I did!" I cried.

"You do."

I grew upset with her now. "No, I don't! If I did, I wouldn't be here."

"You're not aware of it yet, but it's in there, somewhere. Because wherever he is, you are there, too."

"Even if that's true, it doesn't help me right now because I don't know how to access that information. Please, just tell me what you know."

Minerva released my hand, and refocused her concentration on the trophy, closing her eyes and starting to sway and mumble. After ten minutes of this, she emerged again with her usual bizarre "Hello, girls" greeting, and told us what she knew.

"He is in the Underworld, in a prison of mirrors, if I heard that part right. One of my guides who is able to travel there has located him and told him you are looking for him with my help."

"Well, that's great!" I said. "Isn't it? I mean, knowing where he is makes it easier to help him get back to the Vortex."

"He is there for a reason, but my guides tell me that only his Kindred can get him out. She knows this, the one who keeps him. She is counting on it."

"Why?"

"She wants what you have."

"What do I have that she could possibly want?"

"That's what we have to find out."

"I'm scared," said Kelsey, looking at me. I nodded, because I was, too.

Minerva continued. "The Underworld is most difficult to find, but Clyde can help us." She paused a moment, and stared into my eyes with a serious expression before asking me, "When you died, where did you go?"

I tried to remember. "It was a good place," I said. "Good people were there, and I knew that I was loved. I was very happy there. I didn't want to leave."

"The Afterworld," said Minerva. "You are good, and pure, and we are fortunate to know this, as it bodes well for helping Travis. That, plus you being of the world of the living. With my help, you will be able to access the seventh level of the Underworld, and travel there, and if you are careful, find Travis."

I was filled with excitement, but also dread and fear.

"How will I get there?" I asked. "Will it be in dreams, or in my real physical body?"

Minerva grew somber. "The Underworld is a real physical place, Shane. It's not some fairy dust fantasy. It exists, but not in our dimension here in life on Earth as we know it. But you can get there."

"A portal?" I asked.

"Yes. A shortcut through space and time, a cosmic tunnel. You will have to get there in your real and physical self, because until and unless you are dead, your spirit cannot be separated from your body. Do you understand? To send only your spirit would be to kill yourself now."

I nodded.

"You mentioned to me that you knew of a wormhole, or portal as you called it," she said. "You saw Travis use one."

"Yes!" I told her in detail about the cavern near Chaco Canyon, and her eyes grew wide with wonder and excitement.

"I have heard for years of such places, and I have sensed it when I was near one, but I have never been fortunate enough to see one for myself. Shane, if you will let me, I will accompany you on the journey to find Travis."

"Can you do that?"

She nodded. "It is riskier for me, because I do not have a Kindred—at least not that I know of—on the other side to help strengthen my energy once I am there. But I have my guides and my many connections, and I have knowledge of things that, while not perfect in any way, shape, or form, is certainly more than you might have entering such a foreboding and unforgiving place on your own."

"How long would we be gone?" I asked.

"I don't know, Shane. I'm honestly not sure how that would work. We could be gone for what feels like a very short time here, but it would feel like a very long time there, or vice versa. It's uncharted territory."

"Would we be able to get back?" I asked.

"I would most certainly make sure that we could."

I looked at Kelsey, and she seemed worried. "You don't have to do this," she said. Looking at Minerva, she said, "Right? She doesn't have to do this."

"No, you don't have to do this," Minerva told me. "We can try to deal with the dark mark upon you in other ways, through spiritual cleansing and through ceremonies to ward off any more evil spirits. We can protect you as best we can, and you can try to continue with your life as you knew it before. There is danger in that as well, but it is not beyond the realm of possibility. I can help you, if that's the route you wish to go."

I shook my head vehemently. "No. There's no way I'm leaving him there, not if there's a chance I can help him escape." I began to cry, but the tears were hot with purpose and conviction. "He saved me, and it is up to me now, to save him. I feel it. I need to do this."

"Are you quite sure?" Minerva asked me, but her eyes glowed with approval. She knew this was the right thing to do, viscerally, just as I did.

"Absolutely," I said. Kelsey looked uncertain, and upset.

"Very well," Minerva said, dusting her hands together as though we were coming up with a plan to bake a pie.

"Then here's what we'll do. We will go see Clyde. We'll get his help. You girls will find a way to make it look like Shane has run away from home. People will fret and search for you, of course," she told me, "but in the end it will all work out just fine." She turned to my friend. "Kelsey, it will be very important for you to keep up this charade for us, darling, you understand?"

Kelsey nodded, fear in her eyes. "I think so."

Minerva stared Kelsey down. "You *think* so? We cannot do it without your cooperation, love. Are you in, or not?"

"In," said Kelsey weakly.

This seemed to satisfy Minerva. "Give me a couple of days to sort this all through and to consult with some people and guides and spirits I know, and I will come up with a plan for us."

"Can I come with you guys?" asked Kelsey.

"No," I said.

"I'm afraid not," said Minerva. "It's far too risky as it is. I cannot reasonably put two young girls in danger, besides which, your energy tells me that you are needed here, for important purposes. We all have a journey, and all of us must honor it to the best of our abilities with as much dignity as we can muster."

"What are the risks of Shane going to the Underworld or Hell or whatever it is?" asked Kelsey, her eyes watering up.

"Worst-case scenario, we don't come back," said Minerva.

"Shane, you can't do this," shouted Kelsey. "I know you love him and he's very special to you, but you have a life here. You can't throw it all away to, to . . ."

Kelsey couldn't finish the thought, so I finished it for her. "To save Travis's soul. That's what I'd be doing."

"Yeah," said Kelsey in defeat. "I know it sounds noble, but I can't lose you. You're my best friend. You have so much to live for. It's not worth it, Shane. It really isn't."

I thought of Travis, and of the powerful love we shared, of the electricity between us, and the fact that he had risked his own soul just to see me one last time, and I said, without hesitation, "Yes, Kelsey, it is worth it."

Acknowledgments

I wish to thank Antonia Markiet, senior executive editor at HarperCollins, for believing in this book from the start, and for editing with diligence, brilliance, and patience. You are one in a million, and I am glad you're mine. Thank you.

I'd also like to thank Jayne Carapezzi, Sasha Illingworth, Tom Forget, and Jessica Berg for their work on this book.